DEMON FORGED

THE CAMELOT ARCHIVE - BOOK THREE

NICOLE R. TAYLOR

1

The sun rose over Camelot, bathing the ruined city in the fire of a new day.

It was unseasonably warm—just last week we'd been expecting snow—though I wasn't complaining. The growing light made the crumbled buildings look mysterious and romantic.

I sat atop a wall in the upper city—otherwise known as the posh part of town—and looked over the inner castle. Once it had been the palace that housed the great Natural king, Arthur Pendragon and his queen, Guinevere…until it was ripped apart and demons flooded into the world.

I wondered what they'd make of us now. Wilder, the last living descendant of the Pendragon bloodline, was the Natural embodiment of Excalibur, just like Scarlett Ravenwood was Arondight—the swords gifted by the Lady of the Lake and tore the world in two.

And me… I wondered what they'd think of

Madeleine Greenbriar and the things she'd done to save Camelot.

I was a Triune—part Natural, part demon, part Druid. It was a lot to take in, but at least it had a name of sorts.

I couldn't believe that my powers were still evolving, bringing with it the fear of losing control. I'd already done so many impossible things—like calling forth molten lava from the earth, altered people's memories, freed Elijah from his possession, and killed a greater demon—and the thought of more was overwhelming.

"How did I know I'd find you here?"

I looked down at the sound of Elijah's voice and smiled at the sight of him. He was so handsome it hurt, and when he looked at me like he was right now… Shivers. Inappropriate ones.

It had been two weeks since Elijah and I had gone to Ben Nevis to confront Ikakantor. We hadn't quite made it, though. The greater demon had met us on the road and flipped our car, totalling it with us inside. Thankfully, Elijah had enough Druidic magic left to heal himself, otherwise… Well, I wouldn't know what to do if I'd lost him.

His hair had grown out a little since he'd returned to Camelot from his rainforest hideout. He usually kept it shaved all over, but I liked the length—it made him look even more roguish than usual.

He looked up at me with his ethereal green eyes and raised his eyebrows. "Everything okay?"

"Yeah," I replied. "I'm just thinking."

"About me, I hope."

"You're hopeless," I groaned.

Elijah climbed up the wall and sat beside me. "Aren't you leaving for London today?"

I watched him swing his feet back and forth, the heels of his boots hitting the wall beneath us. "Yeah, in an hour or so."

Elijah was silent for a moment, then asked, "Are you worried?"

I shrugged. "The archive bothers me."

The archive sat below the upper city and was full of unknown knowledge and power of the Naturals. Things we'd thought we'd lost forever had begun to resurface but with a heavy price. The Dark had bewitched the Naturals to dig it up because at its depths lay a vault they'd do anything to open. They'd even tried to force their way inside Camelot to get to it…until I'd stopped them.

The vault. Everything was about what lay behind those enormous locked doors.

"The vault has been quiet," Elijah said. "You told me so yourself."

"I know, but—"

"Are you feeling sick again?" The leaking energy from it had made me nauseous, but it subsided after I'd killed Ikakantor—that's how I realised I was sensitive to Darkness in the first place.

I shook my head. "No, but that's not what I meant."

"Come here." Elijah tugged me against his side and stroked his hand through my long black hair. "Without

Ikakantor trying to claw his way inside, the power has settled. We've got time to work it out, Madeleine."

I breathed in the leathery scent of his jacket. "What if something happens while we're gone?"

"You don't have to be responsible for *everything*. The Naturals have experts working on sealing the vault. Ramona believes that once it's taken care of, the Twin Flames will wake from their coma."

Masters—my old Light Studies professor from the academy—was the expert working on the barrier, but I worried about his mental state. He'd become obsessive about his work, remaining in the archive for days at a time, forgetting to eat and sleep. It was difficult not to worry about him.

"It's time for us to rest," Elijah added. "We've fought enough for now, don't you think?"

I smiled. "I am a little tired. Too bad Aiden sealed the portal. We could have gone to Barbados."

"It went to Tahiti, actually."

I rolled my eyes. "A tropical beach is a tropical beach."

We laughed, but Elijah's smile faded faster than mine.

"What is it?" I murmured.

"I've been working with Ramona to repair the damage done to my soul," he began, taking my hand in his. His fingers trailed across my knuckles, but he said nothing else.

"They haven't come back, have they?" I asked with a heavy heart. "Your Colours?"

"I was possessed by a shard of Ikakantor's soul for eight hundred years…there'll always be scars in my spirit."

"I don't understand," I murmured. "Your Colours manifested on that road. I saw it."

"What little power I had left depleted when my body healed itself after the crash."

I understood. His soul was too damaged for his power to remain. It lingered under the surface, but they'd lost their ability to charge.

"*Elijah…*"

"It is what it is," he said. "We can keep trying. At least I'm alive and not withering away before your eyes. I like to think I'm a handsome man, but a wrinkly husk isn't attractive, especially when my girlfriend is an eleven."

My heart leapt. "I'm your girlfriend?"

"Controversial, isn't it?" He wiggled his eyebrows. "The last Druid and the only Triune. You think we could have spread around the awesome at least a little. You know, widen the gene pool."

I slapped his arm. "*Smart arse.*"

It seemed his time as a demon had shaped his personality and now that he was free, some echoes still lingered. Though he was stoic and quite thoughtful as a Druid, Elijah had a sharp sarcastic wit as a demon that I found annoying, yet rather attractive. I was kind of glad it had stuck around—his comedic timing was always on point.

"I may not have declared you as a Druid should,

but it still counts." Until he turned serious again, that was.

"The pattern on my arm?" I asked, remembering the geometric shape that crawled up my right arm and sunk into my skin. "I was in your mind."

"Exactly. I should've done that while we were both conscious. Then when I touched you…" he slipped his palm under the sleeve of my jacket and pushed it upwards, "it would come to life." His fingers traced invisible lines. "A holographic declaration of love."

"Stop that," I said, beginning to squirm.

"Am I making you—"

"*Elijah.*"

His lips quirked. "You're beautiful when you flush."

"I'm… I'm not ready for that."

His expression changed, but he wasn't angry, which put me at ease. "Do you want to walk back to base camp?"

"Sure."

We jumped off the wall and landed softly onto the ground below. Elijah might not have his powers, but he was light on his feet and could hold himself in a fight. Some skills never went away, no matter what arcane abilities we had to back them up.

Base camp was alive with activity when we arrived. Tomorrow was the sixth-year anniversary of the Dark Night attacks and while the official proceedings happened in London, Camelot was having its own remembrance ceremony.

It seemed more important than ever to take the

time to pay our respects to those who fell to the Dark on that terrible night.

In the weeks before the Twin Flames closed the rift, nine Sanctums had fallen in a coordinated attack led by the demon hybrid, Mordred—from whom my mutation originated—including London. The Naturals had been scattered, but in the aftermath of the war, we'd rebuilt and then some. Camelot had been returned to us.

As we approached, I spotted Greer and Issac talking beside the convoy of sleek black sedans. Issac still seemed to harbour some resentment towards Elijah over his convoluted past as a demon-hybrid, but he was doing a good job of hiding it. *Mostly*.

When they saw us approach, Issac broke away, leaving us alone with Greer. *Subtle*.

"Your bag has already been taken care of," she told me, seemingly oblivious to Issac's abrupt departure. Turning to Elijah, she smiled. "Though I'm told we don't have yours."

"You want me to come?" He seemed taken aback by the suggestion.

"If you're going to stay with us, then you will benefit from learning a few of our customs. We aren't the same Naturals you once knew."

"Come," I urged. "It will be good to have you there."

He looked uncomfortable being invited to something that usually wasn't for outsiders, but he nodded. "Sure. Give me five minutes?"

Greer smiled and gestured towards camp. "Certainly. We'll wait for you."

I waited until he was out of earshot before I turned to the acting Inquisitor. "That was really nice of you."

"He has nowhere else to go," she replied sadly. "Camelot was once his home as much as it was ours. The Druids will forever be welcomed amongst the Naturals."

I grimaced. I wondered if she'd change her tune if she knew what they'd done to Elijah.

"Come," she said, oblivious to my internal deliberations. "You and Elijah can ride together. I'll share a car with Issac."

I laughed and nodded. Maybe she knew more about what was going on than I'd ever know.

The Sanctum was bustling as Elijah and I walked out of the parking garage and into the main foyer.

Overhead, the elaborate glass dome let the afternoon sun in, filling the space with natural light that bounced off the black marble floor. At the top of the stairs sat a white marble statue of the Lady of the Lake wielding a representation of the sword of Excalibur. The sculpture had been shattered in the Dark Night attacks, but painstakingly restored in the aftermath—as was much of the Sanctum.

"So, this is your infamous Lady of the Lake."

Elijah looked up at the statue, lost in thought. "What does the plaque say?"

"*Let there be Light amongst the Dark*," I replied.

"Catchy." He glanced around the foyer and laughed, the sound echoed off the marble.

"What?"

"Naturals have an unhealthy fixation on weapons." He gestured to the wall-mounted displays of Medieval era swords, shields, and halberds.

I raised my eyebrows. "Well, we both know how much you dislike using them. These are historical relics, you know."

"If this is the entrance, I can only assume what the rest of the place looks like."

"It gets gaudier," I quipped. "This is nothing. Wait until you see the gallery."

"Ah, portraits of pompous twats in ruffled collars. My favourite."

I laughed and knocked my shoulder against his. "There's some beautiful landscapes of Glastonbury and Avalon I'd like to show you. The artists took artistic license, of course."

"Those places were above my pay grade," he said, revealing a grain of his past. "Do you miss the city?"

"When I was first transferred to Camelot, I thought I would. Now, I can't see how I ever managed to fight demons amongst all this chaos."

"So many humans," he mused, "and so few who are special."

"There she is!" I turned to see Jackson stride down the hall towards us with a huge grin on his face.

"I knew you'd worm your way out of trouble, Madeleine. You do have an uncanny knack for it."

I looked at his T-shirt and raised an eyebrow. It said, *Video games ruined my life. Good thing I have two extra lives.* Below the slogan were three pixilated hearts, two red and one white. Unfortunately, the reference went straight over my head.

"I levelled up," I said. "Is that how it goes?"

Jackson laughed. "I'll make a gamer out of you yet."

Elijah cleared his throat.

I snapped to attention and tugged him against my side. "Elijah, this is Jackson. He helped me a lot back when I was mutated. He… Well, he was…" I'd been talking about my mutation so much that I'd forgotten it might be uncomfortable for others.

Jackson grinned and shoved his hand at Elijah. "I was also mutated by funky demon DNA."

Elijah blinked, then shook his hand. "Oh, I see."

"Yep. These days I'm just a regular human, but they let me stick around." He turned to me. "Are you guys busy tonight? There's going to be a welcome dinner in the kitchens at six. It's nothing fancy like the higher-ups are having with their silver spoons and whatnot. Just the riff-raff."

"Riff-raff, huh?" Elijah raised an eyebrow.

"Sure," I said. "It will be good to see everyone."

"Anyway, I'll let you guys get settled," Jackson said. "It's good to see you looking so well, Madeleine." He glanced at Elijah. "It was good to meet you. If you need anything, just let us know."

Jackson moved down the hall, leaving us in peace. Elijah glared after him and shoved his hands into his pockets.

"What?" I demanded.

"It's good to see you looking so well, Madeleine."

"Don't pout, it makes your mouth look like a cat's arse." I flipped my hair over my shoulder. "By the way, Jackson is married, so no need to get jealous."

"Forgive me," he drawled. "My girlfriend is the most beautiful and powerful creature to currently walk the Earth. Sometimes I wonder what she sees in me."

"Is this about your Colours?" I whispered. "Elijah, I don't care what you are or what you have. I care about *who* you are. Nothing will change that."

He narrowed his eyes and picked up our bags. "So, are we staying in separate rooms?"

"Do you *want* to stay in separate rooms?"

"No, but I like to be the big spoon. You take me as someone who'll fight for it."

I rolled my eyes and walked off down the hall. "C'mon. I still have the key to my old room."

"Can we go see your paintings?"

My annoyance faded and I smiled. I had to cut him a little slack, right? He was in a strange place, with people whose ancestors were once his friends, then his enemies, then his friends again—and that was only the tip of the iceberg. It was easy for me to forget the rollercoaster he'd been through these past few months, let alone his entire life. I couldn't fathom suffering through what Elijah had for fifty years, let alone eight hundred.

"Sure," I replied. "Anything you want."

"Anything I want?" Elijah wiggled his eyebrows. "Be careful what you wish for, pretty Triune. I might just take you up on it."

2

That night, Elijah reluctantly followed me to the riff-raff party in the kitchens, lured with the promise of an all-you-can-eat buffet.

I was sure the thought of facing a crowd of Naturals was intimidating for him, and I felt much the same way. Still, it was important we showed our faces around the Sanctum. Allegiances were hard won for people who'd been at war for over eight generations.

The first familiar faces I saw were Romy and Alo's.

They weren't *together* together, but they'd been partners for six years. Both had lost their other halves in the days following the Dark Night attacks. Romy's partner, Martin, had been possessed and mutated by the Dark along with Alo's partner and girlfriend, Valeria. Now they patrolled and fought on the streets of London together.

In a parallel universe, Romy could have been my older sister. She was tall and lithe, her long black hair tied back into a tight braid. Both arms were covered in geometric tattoos which peeked out from underneath her sleeves and the collar of her jacket.

Alo stood an entire head taller than Elijah and was twice as wide—in a muscular wall of steel kind of way. His long hair had been fashioned into dreadlocks and his beard was scraggly, but that was Alo. His intimidating and overbearing presence was balanced by his warm smile and good heart.

"Hey, it's good to see you," Romy said as she hugged me.

Alo ruffled my hair like he would a little sister's.

"Are you sure?" I asked. "You two were mopping up my mess the last time I saw you."

Elijah narrowed his eyes as we spoke, trying to follow our conversation.

"The night you helped me at *Adrenaline*," I whispered to him.

"Oh, are we keeping that a secret?" he asked loudly.

"What's a secret?" Romy asked, her eyes sparkling with interest.

I sighed and nodded towards the two Naturals. "Elijah, this is Alo and his partner, Romy."

"So this is the Druid," Alo said, looking Elijah over with a keen eye. "Not what I was expecting…"

"*Alo*," Romy hissed.

Elijah snorted. "You were expecting me to look like Gandalf from *Lord of the Rings*?"

Alo laughed and slapped him on the back, the

force of the good-humoured blow almost knocking Elijah off his feet.

"C'mon," he said, dragging Elijah away, "I've got plenty of stories about Madeleine I want to tell you."

"Should I be worried?" Elijah threw over his shoulder.

I waved. "Only a little."

I eased back into the crowd, finding a spot of silence as the party milled around me. That's when I realised I wasn't as inconspicuous as I'd hoped.

Everyone was looking at me in between their conversations. I knew these people and they'd never paid any attention to me—not until I'd…well, *you know*. Most of my time at the London Sanctum had either been in the infirmary fighting a demon mutation or as a warrior hellbent on defying direct orders. No one wanted to touch someone like that for fear it'd rub off on them. Now I was somebody, and I achieved a different kind of isolation.

I scanned the kitchens for a familiar face and spotted Esme at precisely the same time she spotted me.

"Madeleine!" She threw her arms around me but was hampered by her extremely pregnant belly.

"*Esme*." I stared at her stomach. "When did this happen?"

"About eight and a half months ago," she said with a sigh. "I'm about to burst and *thank goodness!* Everything is swollen, I have to pee like every five seconds, and sleeping is *impossible* with this thing." She patted her belly. "I just want it to come out already."

"Careful," Jackson declared, sidling up to her. "That thing is my kid."

"I didn't even know," I admitted.

"I was flat, then one day I was carrying around a bowling ball," she told me. "I thought I was going to be lucky and miss out on the stretch marks, but *no*."

"She's excited, she really is," Jackson deadpanned.

"Well, luckily for you," I told her, "you have access to the best Natural medicine in the world."

"It's much better than what those pesky humans can do," Jackson joked.

"Pain-free labour, here I come!" Esme declared. "Now, where's the ice cream? Ugh, I need to sit down."

I chuckled as she shuffled off in search of something to satisfy her cravings.

"She's happy about it, she really is," Jackson said.

"Are you trying to convince me or yourself?"

"A little from column A, and a little from column B."

I laughed and looked across the kitchens. Elijah sat at a table with Romy and Alo, listening to what was likely a highly exaggerated story about my dislike of authority.

"Are you sure he's the right guy for you?"

I narrowed my eyes. "*Jackson.*"

"What? He seems…grumpy." He looked over my shoulder to where Elijah was sitting amongst the assembled Naturals, seemingly oblivious to the stares he was attracting.

"He's been through a lot," I said. "He has every right to be grumpy."

"Just as long as he treats you with respect."

I snorted. "Well, he's a lot better than when he was a demon, believe me."

"Now I'm even more worried."

"No, not like that," I countered. "He lost his powers. He's a Druid, but…"

Jackson's shoulders sagged and his brow furrowed. "Okay, I get it now. He lost everything that made him special and now he can't protect you. Not that you needed protecting in the first place."

"The sentiment is there," I said.

"In that case, forget everything I said. How long has it been?"

"Two weeks."

He clapped his hands together. "There. See? Two weeks isn't long at all. His life is in complete disarray and you're the only constant."

"How did this go from bagging Elijah to piling the pressure on me?"

"Relationships are a partnership, Madeleine." He looked across the kitchens to where Romy was talking at Elijah. *At*, not *to*. He was staring at her blankly while she was off on some tangent. "Right now, he's lost and confused. He may be free of the Dark, but he's going through another battle. He needs you."

I nodded. Elijah had to figure out who he was and that wasn't an easy feat. His journey was no less important than mine.

"I better rescue him from Romy," I said. "Light knows what they've told him about me."

"And I need to go save the ice cream from my wife and unborn child."

I smiled, imaging him chasing around a toddler-sized version of himself. "You really will have your hands full."

"I know," he groaned and moved away. "I have a few weeks to get my fitness up to par."

I laughed and ducked through the throng of people and slid onto the bench next to Elijah.

"And that's how Madeleine beat the weapons instructor to a pulp on her first day at the Sanctum," Alo said.

"And he didn't forgive me for a full year," I added, remembering poor Christian Lassiter, ten years my senior, who'd had his pride seriously dented. "I really made a name for myself."

"I bet he uses it as a claim to fame these days," Romy stated and put on her best Lassiter voice. "I was beat up by Madeleine *before* she was famous."

Everyone burst out into laughter and Alo slapped his big hand onto the table.

"You look uncomfortable," Elijah murmured. "Are you okay?"

"I came to ask you that." I squirmed, shying away from the attention of the other Naturals.

"I'm fine. I can handle the staring and the awkward questions. I have eight hundred years of personal development up my sleeve."

"Eight hundred years?" Romy's mouth fell open as she overheard our conversation.

Elijah smirked at her. "Give or take a few decades."

"I didn't realise I'd be so…popular is all," I told them. "I didn't really think about it. I did those things because I had to, that's all."

"Madeleine, you're a bonafide heroine now," Romy said. "Camelot was the best thing that could have happened to you. Everyone's heard about the things you did to save the city."

"It depends on how you look at it."

"She's modest," Alo said to the others. "We all do what we have to, but sometimes we need to stop and take pride in our work."

"We're looking to you, Madeleine," Romy said gently. "Without Wilder and Scarlett, you're our greatest hope."

I lowered my gaze and searched for Elijah's hand.

Yeah…that was what I was worried about.

The following day, I sat in the gallery—the same gallery where I'd been interrogated only a few weeks ago—with Elijah as the Dark Night remembrance ceremony got under way.

The room was packed to the brim with Naturals —all five tiers of seating taken up by Sanctum personal, their families, friends, and representatives from other outposts and Sanctums around the world.

The morning was filled with speeches and presentations, recollections and hopes for the future, and pomp and ceremony. Elijah listened dutifully, his gaze occasionally raking across the audience. When a singer performed a haunting song about the fall of Camelot in old Scottish Gaelic, he smiled softly.

I knew days like this were important for many survivors, but for me, it was just a reminder of all the things I'd lost…mainly my ordinary life as a Natural. My destiny had been ripped out of my hands and replaced with an impossible burden. I wondered if this was how Scarlett felt when she awoke as Arondight.

"You're not paying attention," Elijah whispered in my ear.

"Some things I don't care to remember."

"It was a difficult time for you, wasn't it?"

I sighed, sinking down a little in my chair. "The biggest problem I thought I'd face was fighting demons—the Wanderers as you call them—and the odd exorcism or two. Not greater demons and hordes of slithering demonic creatures at Camelot."

"Those slithering creatures are what demons used to be before they were forced out of their bodies and into possessing humans to survive."

"I know."

"That we can kill them at all is a feat in itself."

I looked up at him and studied his features.

"What?" he whispered.

"You said 'we'."

He shrugged and looked back towards the dais

where Greer had appeared, ready to give the closing comments. Once she dismissed the gathering, the ceremony would be over and the rest of the day would be for celebration.

Honestly, I kind of wanted to go back to Camelot.

"On behalf of the Regula and the Codex, I would like to welcome you all to the London Sanctum," she began, projecting her voice into the gallery. "Today, we remember those we've lost and those whose memories still live on inside us and within the pages of the Codex." She reached inside her black blazer and removed a purple velvet box. Opening the case, she lifted out a small gunmetal-coloured object.

"This is the Light of the Lady," she said, holding up the shining cold iron medal. Every Natural knew what it looked like—a sword fashioned after the original form of Excalibur with indigo jewels, representing Arondight, inlaid along its blade. "This is our highest honour, awarded for bravery, resilience, and strength against the Dark. On this sixth anniversary of the Dark Night, it is my honour and privilege as acting Inquisitor to present this award to someone who has risen above and beyond their duties as a warrior to our cause. Someone who stood against prejudice and adversity to protect our legacy and people against impossible odds. To do whatever was in her power to protect this Earth and the people who call it home."

My heart leapt into my throat and Elijah took my hand. She didn't mean me, did she? The only thing I'd ever won was a one-way ticket to detention.

"Her deeds will go down in history beside the greatest of our kind. Beside Excalibur and Arondight. Beside Arthur and Guinevere. Beside Lancelot and Galahad…" Greer's gaze scanned the audience before settling on me. "Madeleine Greenbriar, please approach the dais."

I was frozen, stunned into silence. Elijah nudged me with his elbow, and I rose to my feet like I'd been shocked with a bolt of electricity.

I descended the stairs in a daze, the silence deafening as my boots thudded against the marble underfoot. Finally, I stood before Greer, a complete quivering mess.

"Madeleine Greenbriar," she declared as she pinned the medal to the lapel of my jacket. "On behalf of the Codex and the Regula, I am honoured to award to you the Light of the Lady."

"I don't know what to say…" I murmured as applause erupted around us.

"You don't have to say anything," she murmured.

"I have one hell of a legacy to uphold." I grimaced, the attention making me uncomfortable.

"Follow your heart, Madeleine. It hasn't led you astray…*yet*." Greer smiled and gestured to the dais as the applause peered out. "They're waiting for you."

I swallowed hard and turned, my hands shaking. I could face Ikakantor with nothing but my bare hands, yet public speaking made me want to throw up? *The irony.*

"I just did what any of us would have done." I looked down at the medal pinned to my jacket and wasn't sure how to feel about it. I was proud, I supposed, but I wasn't allowing myself to feel it, not yet.

"This medal isn't just mine," I went on. "It belongs to every single Natural there ever was," I found Elijah in the audience, "and every Druid. It belongs to everyone who fights for what's important. *Life*."

The Naturals began to cheer and clap, filling the gallery with a cacophony of sound that echoed around, all the way up to the glass dome overhead.

I turned to Greer and she shook her head in amusement. I must've said something they liked.

"Will you stay for a moment?" she asked. "There's someone I'd like you to see."

I drew in a sharp breath, my heart swelling. *The Twin Flames*. "Do you mean…? Are they…?"

Greer nodded. "They're here."

3

I held onto Elijah's hand for dear life as we strode through the Sanctum.

His gaze darted about the hall as we ventured into a new part of the building. "Where are we going?"

Three stories down from the main floor sat another kind of vault. Mainly used as cells, this part of the Sanctum was heavily fortified and contained from the outside world. The walls were coated in a layer of cold iron that was polished to a high shine and woven with state-of-the-art security.

"We're visiting some important people," I replied, keeping my voice down.

"Your fiery friends?"

I nodded.

"And they're letting me in?" He let out a low whistle. "*Wow.* How I've risen in the world."

"I don't know if this is a reward or if they think you and I can help given your past and my powers, but I'm grateful I've been given the chance."

Elijah nodded, glancing at the backs of the guards in front of us. Greer walked a few paces in front of them, her almond-coloured hair swishing back and forth.

"You were close?" he murmured.

I nodded. "Scarlett saved my life."

"How do you feel about her now? I mean, she made you what you are."

"I haven't seen her in five years," I replied. "I don't know how I feel."

Elijah fell silent, allowing me to mull it over in my head. Wilder and I had our issues—most of them to do with his cold iron fist of authority. With Scarlett, it was more difficult to pinpoint.

She'd been such a fixture in my life, from saving my soul to helping with my recovery to being there when I struggled through the final months of my training at the Academy. She was the big sister I never had. She was my hero, my idol, and she'd just vanished. It was the nature of our work as Naturals, and more so for her being Arondight, but her absence struck deep.

Absence wasn't the right word, but I couldn't bring myself to admit that I felt abandoned. It would be selfish of me. Scarlett's destiny was not her own.

We came to a halt outside a door and Greer gestured to the guards to wait outside.

"Madeleine." She gestured for me to step forwards.

I dragged Elijah behind me as she opened the door and we entered another world.

One of the larger cells had been converted into something resembling a hospital ward. Machines and various other pieces of equipment lined the walls, as well as a table and two armchairs, but the decor wasn't registering in my brain.

Wilder and Scarlett lay side by side in matching beds with cream and white coloured blankets pulled up to their chests. Their arms lay on top, and wires and electrodes ran from their pale skin, joining up with various machines.

My gaze lingered on Scarlett as I approached. Her brilliant purple hair splayed across the white pillow, vivid as the day I first met her, but she looked sunken as if her coma had burned all of Arondight's Light out of her.

Next to her, Wilder's strong physique had suffered much of the same effects. Seeing the mighty Excalibur appear so fragile was shocking.

My hand flew to my mouth, stifling a whimper. I knew they were in a coma, but seeing it was an entirely different thing.

"It's confronting, I know," Greer said. "But they're in perfect physical health. It's their Light that's dulled."

"Where was she when—"

"She was in Australia when she fell ill," Greer said. "An outpost found something in the outback that needed investigating."

I snorted. "For five years?"

"It's not that simple," she said gently as another man walked into the room. "Madeleine, this is Dr.

Ambrose, a specialist from our Los Angeles Sanctum. He's overseeing Wilder and Scarlett's care."

I looked at the doctor, measuring his worth. Tall with intelligent eyes, wrinkles, salt and pepper hair. He was the image of a studious physician, but was he good?

He seemed to pick up on my cold assessment and smiled. "I can assure you, Miss Greenbriar, that we are taking your friends' care extremely seriously. That's why we've invited you here today."

"I knew it," I muttered. "This wasn't a reward or a compassionate outreach. You want something."

Greer placed her hand on my arm. "If you can help them like you did Elijah and Amanda, then they might wake, or perhaps you might find a way we can help them."

I nodded, shoving my resentment away. I wanted them back just as much as everyone else did…maybe even more. My personal struggles meant nothing.

"Wilder was… He almost seemed afraid of me," I told them. "He thought the Dark was taking over my soul and I'd end up destroying everyone."

"He didn't have time to understand," she said. "They were sick before you were able to grow your abilities."

"No," I shook my head, "it's not that."

Greer glanced at Elijah.

"She's worried she'll do more harm than good," he told her and Dr. Ambrose. "She can change people's memories, which is a rather simple thing to do by accident."

"I did it to Issac," I admitted. "Fortunately, he was aware enough to stop me from making it permanent. It had to be sheer luck I didn't do the same to Amanda."

"Don't undersell your abilities, Madeleine," Elijah told me. "I believe in you."

My hands began to tremble, and I looked down at Scarlett. "I'm not even sure I can make contact."

"Issac can guide you," Greer said. "The mind is his speciality and you know one another."

I looked to Elijah.

He lowered his gaze. "He can help you with this… I cannot."

"I'll send for him." Greer walked over to the door and leaned out, giving an order to one of the guards.

"What if I can't do it?" I whispered to Elijah.

He smiled and smoothed a strand of inky black hair behind my ear. "But what if you can?"

"I guess I'm about to find out."

"*That's the spirit.*"

Issac came at once. He stepped into the room and his gaze fell onto Wilder and Scarlett. From his expression, it was clear this was the first time he'd seen them in person, too.

His gaze flickered to me before settling on Greer. "You sent for me, Inquisitor?"

She nodded and relayed her intentions. Entering the mind of a Flame wasn't exactly an everyday occurrence, and he seemed taken aback as if it was sacrilege. Still, Issac agreed to help. If I was standing here, they had probably run out of options.

"How is her ability different than ours?" Ambrose asked, glancing at me. He'd obviously heard tales of the things I'd done, but his skepticism was high. Maybe he was a good doctor after all.

"We can all see memories we choose to share with one another," Issac explained. "Madeleine can see what we hide away and change it. She can go where our soul meets our consciousness."

I never saw it that way, but I guess he was right. I'd had to cut Ikakantor's essence out of the deepest part of Elijah's consciousness. I hadn't realised it until now, but I'd seen his soul—just as Scarlett had seen mine.

"A demonic ability," the doctor remarked.

Issac frowned, beginning to look annoyed. "In a sense, the ability is similar to a greater demon's, but her Druidic and Natural essence far outweigh any influence the Dark may have on her intent."

"I may be cautious as I am the only one of my kind, but I'm standing right here," I declared. "If you have a question about my abilities, *doctor*, you can ask me directly."

Ambrose coughed and straightened his white jacket. "Very well, then."

"You tell him." Elijah chuckled and straightened the medal on my coat.

"Madeleine has the blessing of the Regula regardless of outside opinion," Greer said, her eyes sparkling with amusement. "Proceed."

Issac turned to me. "Are you ready?"

I nodded and sat on the chair beside Scarlett's bed.

"We'll be here monitoring you both the whole time," Dr. Ambrose said. I guess he had a shred of professionalism after all. "If anything happens, we can intervene."

"You've done this before," Issac murmured, drawing my attention to him. "Ease into her mind and take gentle steps. Experience her memories, but don't merge with what you see. In those moments, it's not about what you would do."

"How do I speak with her?"

"The same way you found me," Elijah replied. "Find a way through her memories to find where she's hiding."

Issac's eyes narrowed slightly, but he nodded. "There'll be a path, but it may not be clear at first. You'll know when you've found her subconscious. You can speak with her there."

"Okay. I'm going in." I slid my hand into Scarlett's and closed my eyes.

I reached out with my power and was relieved to find hers still active. Arondight was there, writhing around Scarlett's Natural Light, but the glow was faint.

Using the tendril, I followed the path into her mind.

***

I was standing in a waiting room.

Looking around, I saw posters promoting various health conditions—tips for avoiding the common cold, how to stop the spread of germs, and vaccination reminders for rubella and measles. It was a doctor's office or hospital.

The room was full of chairs with garish upholstery, dog-eared magazines, and one of those old-fashioned square televisions mounted high in one corner. It had been designed for heavy traffic, but the space was empty of people…save for one.

A little girl with purple and brown pigtails sat on the worn carpeted floor, playing with a set of battered building blocks. She couldn't be more than three or four years old, but I knew her straight away. Her soul had touched mine and I'd recognise it forever, no matter what.

Scarlett.

I took a step forwards as she stacked the blocks on top of one another in one giant tower. When it became unsteady and toppled, she began to build again.

"Scarlett?" I knelt before her, awed at the intelligent spark in her eyes.

She looked up at me and held out a red block with the letter 'M' on it.

"Yes," I said. "M for Madeleine."

Scarlett laughed and shook her head. "Block!"

She set it on the carpet and selected the next one —a green letter 'O'.

"Scarlett, I need to talk to you. Can you show me the way?"

The little girl ignored me and placed a blue letter 'R' onto the tower. She quickly added a pink letter 'G'.

I reached out and placed my hand over the tower. "Scarlett, I've come to help wake you, but you need to listen to me."

Her little brow furrowed and she pouted. "*Block.*"

"Scarlett, *please.*"

She sighed and jabbed a chubby finger towards the darkened corridor.

"Thank you." I rose and smiled down at her. She really was a cute kid with her purple pigtails and single syllable replies.

As soon as I began to walk away, she went straight back to building her little tower of blocks.

I stood at the mouth of the corridor. The light from the waiting room filtered into the opening, but the linoleum floor and beige-coloured walls faded into darkness. A fluorescent tube buzzed and clicked, then flickered overhead.

I guess this was the way forwards. My boots thudded against the linoleum floor as I left the waiting room. The light faded, but I put one foot in front of the other until the nothingness began to clear.

I emerged from the shadows, finding myself at the base of Camelot's ruined inner castle.

It was night. A thousand million stars shone overhead, and the full moon coated the vista with a haunting silver glow. Directly in front of me sat a chasm of unfathomable depths and I peered over the edge. I recognised the telltale signs that let me know a portal rippled below and my heart skipped a beat.

So this was the rift that had brought war to our world.

I shivered and wrapped my arms around my middle. Wilder and Scarlett must have jumped into it when they went to face the One the day they fought to close the way between worlds for good.

This was so a test.

"Scarlett?" I called out. "Are you really going to make me jump?"

My voice echoed off the twisted remains of Camelot and bounced back at me, but there was no other reply.

"She's making me do it," I muttered. "Okay, then."

I looked over the edge and took a deep breath. What did people say before they leapt off something impossibly high? Geronimo?

Here goes nothing.

I jumped.

Wind ripped past my face as I descended through the shadows, then I was spat out into an alien landscape. I landed on a stone path, the sound of my boots muffled in the closeness of the heavy atmosphere.

Huge blocks of stone hovered in the air by an invisible force, and the sky was tinted with the fire of an intense sunset. Time and space didn't seem to matter here, nor the laws of gravity.

My hair began to float as if it I was submerged in

water, though I was able to stand upright and move normally. It was a strange sensation—the air was light, though I was still heavy.

Ruins stretched before me and when I looked up, I saw chunks of earth hovering like tiny islands in the sky beyond the floating blocks.

This must be the place between worlds where the Twin Flames defeated the One. I'd read about it in Scarlett's addition to the Codex but seeing it within her memories was something else entirely.

I took a step down the path and I clapped my hands over my ears as a voice boomed, "State your business!"

It didn't sound like Scarlett. "Scarlett? It's Madeleine!"

"*The way is closed…*"

Screw that. I was the Triune and I was here to get my friend back.

"Too bad," I said, striding forwards. "I'm opening it."

I forged ahead, my feet becoming heavier the farther I progressed down the path. A raised platform emerged from the haze and a shadowy human form materialised.

Scarlett.

I waded through invisible sludge, my boots dragging over uneven cobblestones. Finally, I managed to climb the stairs and she turned, recognition flooding her features.

"Madeleine?" She stared at me in shock. "What are you doing here?"

"You're in a coma, Scarlett. I've come to wake you," I replied. "I've come to bring you home."

"You can't." Scarlett shook her head, her indigo hair fluttering in the strange atmosphere.

"I'm different now. I can do things I've only dreamed of. When you saved my soul, you created a new version of me—Light, Dark and Druidic."

"I know what's happened to you," she told me, her words feeling anticlimactic to the extreme. "I can see it when I look at you. You're alight with colour, Madeleine, but it's not enough."

My brow furrowed. "What are you saying?"

"I now understand why the Lady of the Lake had to leave our world for Avalon." She grasped my shoulders, her fingernails biting into my skin. "We can't exist in the same time and space."

"You…you can't exist?" My lips were moving, but no sound was coming out. An icy wind rose around us, whipping our hair in all directions.

"Has she returned?" When I didn't answer, Scarlett shook me. "Madeleine, *has she returned?*"

I blinked. *The Lady of the Lake?* I shook my head, no.

"Good, then you have time. Listen to me, Madeleine. She cannot set foot in this world, do you hear me? Whatever you do, *don't let her come back.*"

Indigo Flame wrapped around her and she shoved me away, pushing my consciousness out of her mind with all the force she could muster.

With a cry, I snapped back to reality. I shot to my

feet, pushing the chair away with the backs of my legs as I gasped for air.

"Madeleine?" Elijah held me steady as my head spun. "What happened?"

We can't exist in the same time and space. We. The Twin Flames.

It all made sense now. The energy in the vault wasn't a relic or a power source. It was the same kind of creature that created the entire race of Naturals. It was exactly like the Lady of the Lake—a god of unfathomable power.

A celestial being.

Holy shite.

Elijah shook me. "*Madeline.*"

"Camelot," I croaked, grasping his arm. "We have to get back to Camelot. *Now.*"

4

The sleek black sedan careened through the inner city streets of London with Elijah behind the wheel.

How that happened was beyond me, but he drove like an MI6 agent on acid who'd just qualified for pole position at the Monaco Grand Prix.

"Whoo boy, I've missed the thrill of being bad." He spun the wheel to the side, weaving through traffic like a demon—pardon the pun.

"Just don't kill us before we get out of London," I hissed, gripping the seat.

Greer was in the back with Issac, their heads flopping back and forth as the car shot through the narrow streets.

"Thompson, it's Greer," she said into her mobile phone. "We need to secure the vault. Get Masters out of there and await our arrival." She fell silent while he replied. "Don't question me. Get Aiden and evacuate the archive." Another break. "Madeleine went into

Scarlett's mind and spoke to her. *Someone is in that vault trying to get out. There—*" She hissed as Thompson interrupted her. "Yes, Masters may be compromised. Evacuate the city and fall back to base camp *immediately*. We'll be there as soon as we can. Keep me updated on the proceedings." She grimaced as she was cut off again. "There's a bloody celestial being imprisoned underneath Camelot, don't argue with me, Thompson. *Just do it.*"

An easy way to tell how dire things were was when Greer resorted to swearing.

"You should have taken a left there," Issac said.

"This way is faster," Elijah replied. "The M40 bypasses all the big cities and there's fewer police."

I didn't even ask.

"The vault is still locked," I said. "We've got time, but I don't know how much."

"What else did Scarlett say?" Greer asked, taking the focus off Elijah's reckless driving and back to the mission at hand.

"Not much. She pushed me out of her mind before I could ask anything else." I frowned, thinking about the things I'd seen in her subconscious. "She was inside the rift…like she couldn't exist in her mind without going to another world. It was strange."

"We always thought it was the power leaking from the vault that made them sick," Issac said. "But not like this."

"We know nothing about the Lady of the Lake or what she is," Greer mused. "If this creature is like her, then I don't know what to do about it."

I glanced at Elijah, but he kept his eyes on the road. His brow was creased, and I wasn't sure if it was from concentration or concern. If Greer, the leader of our people and protector of the Codex, didn't know what do if the vault opened, then we were in more trouble than we realised.

"I just wish I had time to speak to Wilder." I sighed, but there was no use fretting over it.

"I know, but thanks to you, we could hear Scarlett's warning," Greer told me.

"What are we doing when we get there?" Elijah asked, checking the mirrors as he merged onto the motorway. "I get the feeling we're going to be driving onto another battlefield."

"We will meet with Aiden and Thompson and work on our next steps," Greer replied. "For now, they are evacuating and erecting a temporary barrier around the archive."

"We have to be prepared for anything," Issac stated, placing a hand on my shoulder from behind.

"I don't know what I can do," I scoffed. "I mean, I can do stuff… but not like a Flame."

"Let's not get ahead of ourselves," Greer said. "Let's just worry about getting back to Camelot."

"Was that code for 'step on it'?" Elijah quipped. "Because your wish is my command!"

He planted his foot on the accelerator and we sped up, hurtling across the English countryside like a rocket. I hoped he was right about the police.

"I think I liked him better as a demon," Issac muttered. "He had an excuse for being an ar—"

"*Issac*," Greer hissed.

Elijah glared at him in the rearview mirror. "*Pòg mo thòin.*"

"What does that mean?" I asked, knowing full well it was for mature audiences only.

"It means exactly what you think it does." He smirked and flashed me a wink. "It's Irish for *kiss my arse.*"

Camelot was in full lockdown mode when the car sped through the wards and into the field beside the base camp.

Aiden and his brother, Thompson, came to meet us as we got out. They looked flustered, but so did everyone. Warriors assembled in teams, manning the walls and assisting with the non-combat personnel.

"Where's Masters?" Greer asked.

"We had to restrain him," Thompson replied. "He started ranting and raving and tried to attack the guards."

"I had to drag him away from the vault," Aiden added. "He wouldn't come, but he's with Ramona in the infirmary."

"Was there anything wrong with the vault door?" Greer asked.

"No, not that I could see, but that thing is an elaborate puzzle of gears and cogs. If there was, it'd be impossible to tell."

"My nausea was rising," I said to her.

"Remember? When we came back from the rainforest, I could feel it all the way up in the foyer."

"I don't think Masters was working on a barrier," Issac said.

"He was influenced by whoever's behind that door," I finished. "Ikakantor tricked us into opening the archive and that's all it took to wake the creature in the vault."

Greer paled and whispered, "The Dark wanted this all along."

"We have to seal the archive," Thompson said. "Fill in the entrance and never open it again."

Elijah grabbed my arm. "Can you feel that?"

I stilled and looked at the ground. A low vibration hummed through the earth before it began to tremor through my boots.

"The ground is shaking," I said.

"An earthquake," Greer murmured. "Hold steady."

In the city above, the castle exploded, the blast sending stone and debris into the air. A split-second later, a fireball followed, billowing into the sky like an atomic bomb's mushroom cloud. It crackled with unearthly energy, shimmering crimson as it dissipated.

A shape emerged from the flame, twisting and turning, then it began to rain destruction down onto the ruins of Camelot. Buildings exploded, throwing stone and ash into the air. The booms of multiple explosions echoed down the valley to base camp, triggering panic as debris started to fall.

The warriors corralled the terrified scientists and

academics, sheltering them behind a barrier of Light that flared gold as rock pelted the camp. The rushed defences were holding…for now.

"Holy shite," Aiden exclaimed, pointing towards the upper city. "It's a woman."

"*My god*," Issac breathed, "she's a Celestial…"

Scarlett's plea echoed in my mind and I cursed under my breath. *Listen to me, Madeleine. She cannot set foot in this world, do you hear me? Whatever you do, don't let her come back.* It was too late for that now.

"We have to try to talk to her," Greer said. She understood, too.

"She's tearing apart the city," I declared. "I think we're beyond negotiating at this point."

"If we can calm her down and get her on side, we could understand what she wants," Issac told me. "She might not be our enemy."

I took a step forwards. "Then I can try to talk her down and see what she wants. If she attacks, I have the power to protect myself."

"I will go," Greer said. "I am the highest authority."

"Do you really want to go up there?" Issac asked. "She could kill you and where would we be then? No Codex. No Inquisitor. We'd be lost."

"We'd have you, Issac," she murmured.

He blinked. "What?"

"If anything happens to me, I want you to assume the role of acting Inquisitor in my stead."

"What about the Codex?" I asked.

"It will choose a new protector." She made it sound so simple.

"That is a load of steaming bullshite," Elijah declared. We all turned to stare at him, but he was watching the Celestial rain hellfire down on Camelot. "You're arguing about being martyrs while your precious castle burns. Madeleine has the power to protect herself. I don't want her to go, but she has the best chance for survival. Doing nothing is not an option. Sacrificing the leader of an entire race of people is a bad idea." He glanced at Issac and shrugged. "But what would I know, I used to be a demon."

"You're a Druid," I said. "Druids once advised the Naturals." I turned to the others. "I'm going, even if I have to defy orders."

"Yeah, it's her favourite pastime," Elijah added.

"Go," Greer said with an abrupt nod. "Be safe."

I squared my jaw and took off through base camp, sprinting past buildings, worksites, and tents. Passing through the barrier, I entered the lower city.

Flaming rock fragments rained down and I was forced to dodge the molten debris as I made my way up the thoroughfare to the castle.

It looked like a war zone. I mean, I'd raised lava from the earth itself outside the city walls, but this was a whole other level. The destruction had no rhyme or reason to it. It felt like an epic temper tantrum to me.

Skidding to a halt near the courtyard before the castle gates, my gaze flicked across the scene ahead. Smoke billowed from a massive hole in the roof of the archive, and I knew Aiden would be heartbroken. All his work had disintegrated in a blink of an eye.

Ash fell from above, fluttering through the air like snowflakes. The stone wall had melted in places, molten rock dripping down the façade.

The Celestial floated in the sky, a ball of pure rage, and she descended as her anger abated, landing before the broken gates of Camelot's inner bailey.

She was naked as the day she was born, and her ivory skin had been smeared with dirt and ash. She appeared human, but I felt the waves of energy radiate around her, though the nausea I'd felt inside the archive wasn't present. *Curious…*

The woman seemed dazed, like she was seeing the world for the first time. Her long black hair cascaded down her back in waves and fluttered as she turned.

Our gazes met and I froze, my breath catching. I could see forever and beyond etched into her irises. Infinity.

She was a phoenix that had risen from the ashes.

"Hello?" I murmured. The sound of my voice echoed across the courtyard, the scene harkening back to the memory I'd seen inside Scarlett's mind.

"Where has it gone?" she asked. I couldn't place her accent—it was exotic, yet familiar.

I understood now. She was confused and in pain. Still, she was dangerous and who knew what her intentions were? The Dark wanted to free her from the vault to destroy us, but no one had seemed to ask the million-dollar question that now settled in my mind.

Why was she imprisoned in the first place?

"Where is what?" I asked gently.

"*Camelot.*" Fire traced across her skin, ripping like flame across an oil slick.

"It was destroyed a long time ago," I replied, edging towards her.

She strode towards me, the air shimmering around her. "By whom?"

I was dazed for a moment, then replied, "It's a long story."

Her next movement was so abrupt, I didn't have time to react.

The Celestial's fingers wrapped around my throat and I felt her blazing presence drive into my mind. Pain tore through me and I screamed, the inferno burning me from the inside out.

She was sifting through my memories—learning and adapting—and there was nothing I could do to stop her.

"This was the world she created?" the woman asked. "Ash and ruins?"

"*Please,*" I begged, "we want to talk. *To help…*"

The Celestial tightened her grip and sneered, "*Abomination.*"

She had a point. I shouldn't exist. I was an accident.

"I didn't ask for this," I rasped.

"Then you should have been ended before it was irreversible."

Irreversible? Of course, I couldn't go back, but… "I don't understand."

The woman scoffed, "They don't understand what they've created. *Fools.* She left you here without guidance like the irresponsible child she always was and scurried off into her secret universe to hide. *Pathetic.*"

She roared in anger and hurled me across the courtyard. I collided with the melted wall and landed face down onto the pooled rock.

"You don't know what true power is," she raved, her body igniting in iridescent red flame.

She shimmered like stardust, but all I saw was the rage bottled up inside her, ready to blow. There was going to be no negotiation, just destruction.

I grimaced as I pushed to my feet but my gaze never left the Celestial as her flame intensified. There was a fight coming and I was likely going to my death, but I had to protect the people below.

The Celestial fixed her attention on me as I moved. I wrenched my arondight blade from my belt and the sword sprang into life, showering red and silver sparks across the courtyard.

"Pretty." The woman laughed as she watched the arcane flame wrap around my sword. "Your courage is admirable, but ill advised." She lifted her palm, her fingers moulding a ball of living flame. "Mine is better, don't you think?" Her expression twisted and she hurled her creation at me.

Raising my blade, I deflected the flame and advanced, but she had more. I cut to the left then the right, ducked and weaved. Fire burned my skin, but I pushed through the pain tearing at my flesh.

The few paces it took to close the space between us felt like miles, but she was within reach soon enough. I brought down the arondight blade, swinging with all my strength.

The Celestial's hand shot up and wrapped around the sword, the impact jarring up my arms. My eyes widened in shock as she wrenched the weapon from my grasp and flung it across the courtyard. Metal clattered on stone as the blade retracted and my head snapped to the side.

I didn't even see the blow, but the force sent me to my knees. I gasped, my vision blurring as I collapsed over the remains of the mosaic crest of the Pendragon's of Camelot.

I'd never felt pain like this—numbing and blistering all at the same time.

I was dying.

I could feel it in my soul, but even as the life slipped from my body, it crept back in from my spirit like an ouroboros—the serpent eating its own tail.

Elijah was right…

"You fought admirably for an abomination, but there will be no victory for you." The Celestial stood over me, alive with living flame, her hair floating in an ethereal halo around her face. "Deliver a message to your kind, Madeleine Greenbriar, and know my mercy."

I coughed and tasted the metallic tang of blood on my tongue.

"I am Morgana," she said, standing tall. "I am made of the universe and the forces that created time itself. It would do you well not to forget the power I hold. Your people will atone for the pain they forced upon me."

She ignited and rose into the air, her bare feet lifting off the mosaic.

Morgana.

I watched in awe as she shot towards the heavens, the glow of her flame dimming until she reached the upper atmosphere. My eyes fluttered closed as she disappeared amongst the stars.

And we thought the Dark was bad…this was worse.

Much worse.

5

———

Dreams filled my mind with shadows and spectres.

A nightmarish landscape wrapped around me, its barbs dragging against my skin and tearing me open.

I died and was reborn again and again. I didn't know many times I circled around myself. Time was infinite.

Reality twisted and finally, I opened my eyes.

The first sensation I felt was softness. I was in bed, my listless body sinking into an unknown mattress. Then the smells of antiseptic and freshly laundered sheets.

The infirmary.

My gaze flickered around the room. My arondight blade sat on the side table, along with the Light of the Lady medal. It had remained pinned to my jacket, forgotten in all the chaos, but now it sat proudly beside my sword. The honour seemed hollow after my epic fail with Morgana.

"Madeleine?" Elijah's hand found my face and he stroked his thumb across my cheek.

I had to tell them.

"She knows everything," I rasped, my throat little better than sandpaper. "My power was useless."

"*Shh*," Elijah crooned, his eyes soft. "It's okay. You need your rest."

"She drove into my mind and took… She…"

He froze, his brow creasing. "The Celestial?"

"Morgana," I whispered. "Her name is Morgana and… *Revenge*."

"Revenge?"

My head throbbed as I nodded. "On us."

Elijah frowned and pressed his palm against my forehead.

"I'll tell them," he said. "Don't worry about anything, okay? Just rest."

"I should be dead." My eyes drooped as unconsciousness tugged at my mind. "You were right."

A moment of silence followed before he spoke again. "It seems so."

"Where is she?" A dull pain throbbed through my head, the feeling of helplessness unfamiliar. I wasn't used to my strength being taken from me.

"Gone," Elijah replied.

"Gone?"

"There's no trace of her."

"She'll be back," I whispered as I descended into another round of restless sleep. "*You'll see.*"

Sometime later, I woke amongst the shadows of night.

Elijah was draped in a chair beside the bed, his body hunched forwards against the mattress. His head rested against his elbow as he dozed.

I lifted my hand and threaded my fingers through his chestnut hair. In the absence of a pair of clippers, it had grown a full inch.

He stirred at my touch and his head lifted. "Madeleine?"

I smiled, groggy from sleep. "I'm okay."

His hand found mine and he lifted it to his lips. The soft brush of his kiss warmed me and a tired smile tugged at the corners of my mouth.

"I couldn't help you," he whispered.

"No one could have," I told him. "Don't beat yourself up about it."

I stared out the window and across the infirmary to where Ramona was fussing over Masters. Everything made sense now, but I wasn't sure knowing how we'd gotten to this point was going to help with the battle to come.

Morgana's escape was inevitable. Her power was absolute and nothing could stand against her. Arondight and Excalibur were out of play and even my strange new abilities weren't enough. She'd struck me down without even lifting her hand.

"She knew I couldn't die," I said. "I was the perfect messenger. If Greer had gone instead of me…" I squeezed my eyes closed.

"I regret sending you up there."

My eyes flew open. "No. This was no one's fault. I wanted to go. I was the only one who could."

"I still regret it."

"This is my life, Elijah. Fighting and risking myself came with being a Natural. Nothing has changed just because I'm a Triune. I was born to protect this world."

He lowered his gaze. "I know. It's just a bitter pill to swallow."

"There's a chance we might never know peace," I whispered. "But we fight anyway, knowing we're the only ones who can."

"I can see why the Druids lived amongst your people."

"You talk about them like you weren't one."

Elijah grimaced and lowered his gaze. His people had abandoned him, so I couldn't blame him for wanting to distance himself.

"When I found you up at the castle…"

"I'm okay," I urged, a pang striking me in the heart. His level of distress for my wellbeing was strange and unfamiliar, but not entirely unwelcome.

"Thanks to your powers."

"Where are the others?" I asked.

"Talking about what they're going to do next," he replied with a shrug. "Mainly, they're yelling at one another."

"I'm not surprised," I drawled. "No one could have known what was in the vault."

"Greer said she should have let you see the Twin

Flames sooner."

"It's no use thinking about should haves," I told him. "What about the camp?"

"Tense. No one was injured, but your archeologist friend is up in arms about the damage to the archive."

I groaned. "Aiden will be devastated. Was much lost?"

"The Celestial blew a hole right through the centre of the whole building," Elijah told me. "The vault door melted into a big puddle of gold and silver. A lot of artefacts were lost and the portals are gone."

"Gone?"

"The explosion untethered them from their anchors. If anyone steps into them from the other side, they'll end up on a long road to nowhere. They're useless now."

I sighed. At least no one was hurt, but Camelot was even more of a smoking ruin that it had been before.

But if Morgana came back or lashed out at humanity, the entire planet could become an uninhabitable fiery pit of Hell. What did the humans call it in their Hollywood disaster movies? An extinction level event.

I grimaced and flung the blankets off me. I swung my legs out of bed, but Elijah placed his hands on my shoulders.

"Hey," he murmured, "no heroics today. Back into bed with you."

"I can't stay here when—"

"You can," he interrupted. "Ramona said that

whatever Morgana attacked you with burned your spirit. It needs time to repair itself."

"Burned my spirit?" I raised my eyebrows. That was a new one. I'd never heard of a soul being burned before. Drained, yes—that was soul sickness. Burned? No.

"Druids know a lot about spirits," he told me. "If I could access my Colours, maybe I could help…"

"You know a lot of strange things," I said, trying to distract him from his guilt. It wasn't his fault he couldn't regain his former self, but he shouldn't feel inadequate over it. It made no difference to me. "You Druids are so mysterious. Maybe that's why I like you so much."

"Flattery will get you everywhere but out of this bed," he declared. "I can get in with you if you'd like."

"I'd like that."

His gaze became heated and I flushed, sliding my legs back into bed. Standing, he fixed the blanket and climbed onto the mattress beside me on top of the covers. He stretched out his long body and coaxed me to use him as a pillow.

I nestled into the crook of his arm and rested my cheek against his chest. Splaying my fingers across the soft fabric of his T-shirt, I felt the raised lines of the scars that ripped across his flesh. They were forever a reminder of his imprisonment. A mark left behind from the Dark.

Elijah breathed deeply and his free hand traced the length of my arm. If I was going to ask him anything about his past, I supposed now was the perfect time to do it.

"What exactly can a Druid do that a Natural can't?"

"Hmmm…"

"Can you tell me? Or is it a secret?"

"Not so much a secret than a forgotten part of myself," he replied. "I've lived a long time."

"Do you remember much?"

"Fragments. I barely have any recollection from when the Dark was in control, but time can erode memory." He was silent for a moment, the lapse in our conversation enough to let the sounds of the base camp filter in from outside. "Druids can do many of the same things a Natural can, but our power works differently. We can connect with the elements and manipulate them to our will, using the sacred geometry inherent in nature." That seemed to explain the intricate shapes his power had taken while I was in his subconscious.

"That's why you call your spells prisms?"

"Something like that. It's the way our Colours reflect off the shapes we weave."

"What about runes?"

"More angles," he replied with a smirk.

"Trigonometry, eat your heart out. Can you shapeshift, too?"

"It's all the same thing, really. The human body is made up of elemental forces, just like everything else on the planet."

"You didn't answer my question."

Elijah sighed and I knew I'd hit a sore point. "I was young when I was taken. I hadn't yet mastered many of the things a Druid should know."

"But you look like… Well…"

He laughed. "In Druidic terms, I was still a bairn."

I smirked. "A little Scottish baby. You must have been cute when you were a kid."

"I was irresistible."

"Your accent isn't very thick," I mused. "And you don't say many Scottish things."

"Time, travel, and other things changed me, Madeleine. I'm no longer the man I was before."

I tensed. "I guess not."

"I'm still not sure who I am now."

"That's something we both have in common." I looked up at him. His gaze was fixed on the ceiling and I wriggled against him. "It's like you said, we're both evolving."

Elijah looked at me, his emerald eyes simmering. "I guess you're right."

He kissed me, holding our embrace softly. To me, Elijah seemed to be a complex enigma of echoes. I liked all of his facets—which manifested like the Druidic prisms he talked about—though sometimes it was difficult to keep up.

"Can I tell you a secret?" he whispered.

"You can tell me anything."

"I don't think I could have lived with this without you." This, being his lack of power.

"Of course, you could have." I traced the lines of

his jaw. "You're strong."

"I wanted you from the first moment I laid eyes on you in that nightclub. Nothing else matters."

I froze, knowing my uncertainty and inexperience was likely hurting him. Letting go was difficult when the world was out to get me.

"It's okay," he said. "I understand."

"I just… I don't want to be without you."

A sad smile pulled at his lips. "Can I tell you about the day I returned?"

"Of course, you can." I wasn't sure what day he was talking about, but it didn't matter. He was opening up to me and it meant the world. I knew how precious trust could be.

He took a deep breath and drew me close. "I don't care for the little details, so this will be short and bittersweet."

"Tell it however you like. I'm not going anywhere."

We lay together in the dark for a long moment as Elijah gathered his thoughts.

"I remember little from the time I was with the Dark," he began, "just flashes of fragmented memories and echoes of pain. At the time, I wasn't sure if I escaped or if I was set free, but I came to realise it was the latter." He paused, remembering. "I returned to my family, or what was left of it. They were afraid. They could sense the changes in me, even if I couldn't. No one knew what to do, so they presented me to Merlin to see if he could cure me of the Dark's touch."

I already knew they didn't rid him of his possession, but I wondered what Merlin had said. Elijah had been abandoned and left for dead, so it couldn't have been good.

"There was already talk about leaving for the Druid homeland," Elijah continued. "Merlin said he knew the way through the Darklands to the hidden portals. We were ruthlessly hunted and had become nomadic and even more secretive in order to stay ahead of the enemy. There was nowhere else to go in this world but to the next. People were already preparing to leave when I returned. The Dark was too strong, and we were too few. The Naturals couldn't help us—they were just as splintered and decimated as we were. Camelot was gone, the Lady of the Lake had already withdrawn to Avalon, and we were on our own."

"What did Merlin say when you went to him?"

"Nothing," he whispered. "He said nothing."

I clutched him tighter. "Nothing at all?"

"I fell to my knees before him and begged for help. He looked down upon me for a long time before he walked away." Elijah sounded numb. "Everyone followed. I grovelled in the dirt, pleading for help and they turned their backs on me."

"Even your family?"

"Merlin's word was law."

"Who the hell was Merlin to be so cruel?" I spat, my anger rising.

"He was our leader," Elijah told me. "The singular, oldest, and most powerful Druid there ever was. If he couldn't save me, then I was death to all I loved. They had to abandon me or risk losing everything." He sighed, his breath shaking. "It took me eight hundred years to understand, but I would have been the seed of their destruction."

He would have unknowingly led the Dark through the Darklands to the Druid homeland, dooming his people and their world to extinction.

"*Oh, Elijah.*" He didn't let out his emotions, but my tears dampened his T-shirt on his behalf.

"That's what happened," he murmured. "It was a long time ago now."

"It doesn't mean it hurts any less."

"No, perhaps not."

He stroked my hair for a few minutes, lost in the haze of his past.

"I've been selfish," he said, unravelling himself from my grasp. "I best let Ramona know you've woken."

I burrowed amongst the blankets as he stood and walked towards the door, his story simmering in my mind. I was angry for him as though it had happened yesterday, not centuries ago.

"Elijah?"

He paused and looked over his shoulder, the light from the infirmary playing along his strong profile. "Yeah?"

"I'm glad you're okay."

He smiled and shook his head. "That's what I'm supposed to say to you."

6

I stood at the edge of the training yard watching the Naturals move through their daily drills.

A dozen warriors sparred at the far end, practicing their hand-to-hand combat. The rest were stationed on the wall and in the city, patrolling and helping to assess the damage done to the archive.

I leaned against the ancient wall surrounding the yard and sighed. Morgana had disappeared without a trace. There'd been no sightings since she'd flown away from Camelot, but her absence didn't reassure me. She was coming back… we just didn't know when.

"There she is."

I turned just in time to catch Maisy as she flung her arms around me.

I laughed, my heart skipping a beat at her sudden appearance, and we held each other tight. "Maisy, thank the Light."

"Everyone's okay," she said, drawing back. "The

upper city and the castle are a complete shite show, but we can deal with it."

"Just another day then."

She nodded her agreement. "Where's Elijah?"

"Working with Ramona."

"He's still trying to wake up his powers?"

I nodded and glanced up at the castle. "I'm not sure how much good it's doing, but it's important to him."

"Of course. I don't know what I'd do if I lost my Light." Maisy followed my gaze. "What happened up there?"

Memories flashed in my mind—Morgana grasping my arondight blade, the living fire playing across her skin, the strength that had forced me down—and I shook my head. "I'm not sure. It all happened so fast. No one's really said anything about how I got from the castle to the infirmary."

"Well, when the Celestial flew away and you didn't come back, Elijah tore up there like a crazy person. He even outran Issac."

I straightened up. "Elijah?"

"Yeah, you should have seen him," she told me. "When he carried you out of the ruins, we all thought you were dead."

I saw a vision of Elijah carrying my bloody, broken body out of the smoke, his face smeared with ash and tears, and shook my head. He'd never mentioned it, which told me a great deal of the man he used to be and the man he was becoming again.

"How are you, though? Ramona must be pleased if you're out of the infirmary."

"Good as new," I replied. "I was a little bruised on the inside, is all."

"Your soul was bruised?" She must have talked to Ramona about my condition.

"Have you seen Trent?" I asked, changing the subject.

"Subtle," Maisy said with a laugh. "Trent's on patrol."

"Amanda? I felt like I haven't seen her in ages."

"Up at the archive. You know, I think her and Aiden are sneaking around." She made a kissy face.

I mock gasped and began to laugh. "Good for them."

"Yeah, he's the dreamboat who's oblivious about being a dreamboat. At least he bagged another nerd. I don't think anyone else could stand his enthusiasm levels for digging up shards of old pottery."

We were still thoroughly discussing romance when Issac appeared. He stared at us for a moment, then tried unsuccessfully to smother a grin.

Maisy coughed and straightened her uniform—if you could call standard black tactical gear a uniform. "I better get going," she said. "I've got to report to Thompson in ten."

"How are you feeling?" Issac asked as Maisy made a hasty retreat.

I shrugged. "Fine. Distracted maybe, but I feel strong."

"I thought you'd might like to train."

I glanced at the yard and back to him. "Out there or cross-legged on a cushion?"

He laughed and shook his head. "I think we're past meditation, don't you?"

I slipped my arondight blade from the loop on my belt and allowed the blade to engage as I stepped out into the yard.

Issac stood beside me, watching the Light play up and down the cold iron.

"Your Light is changing," he said. "It was red and white, but now it looks almost metallic."

I held up my arondight blade and ran my finger over the cold iron fuller—the groove that ran down the centre of the sword. The flame rippled, glistening like liquid metal. I could see flecks of silver and red, but a new colour had appeared—a subtle smoky blue that appeared when light dappled across it.

"You're right," I said. "Do you think they'll mix?"

"Perhaps. Though I think it's more likely one colour will dominate the others."

I frowned and studied the sword. Would I have a dominate trait amongst the Triune? It was a curious idea.

Issac coughed. "Can I ask you a question?"

"What kind?" I set down my sword and the blade retracted into the hilt.

"Are you happy?"

I blinked. "Am I happy?"

"With Elijah."

I sighed. Now the truth came out. "I know you don't see eye to eye with him—"

"I'm asking about you," he interrupted. "What I think about Elijah is irrelevant."

"It's not when it's the thing that's driving this conversation."

He smiled, his gaze simmering. "I've met my match with you, haven't it?"

"Issac…" My cheeks flushed, but it wasn't because of hidden romantic feelings. We'd already had this conversation.

"Don't worry about it," he said, leaning against the wall. He looked up at the castle and ran his hand through his blond hair. "My feelings are my responsibility."

"They are," a voice said behind us. "And you better keep them away from my girl."

I turned to find Elijah scowling at Issac. *If looks could kill.*

Issac sighed and straightened to his full height. "And what would you do about it?"

"Stop it," I said. "We've been through this."

"He thinks because I'm a Druid with no powers, that I can't fight," Elijah snarled. "Apparently, we're meant to be pacifists with epic protractor skills."

Issac glowered. "History tells us—"

"History is standing in front of you," he snapped. "*Someone give me a sword.*"

"Elijah," I complained. "Really?"

A Natural ran up beside Elijah and handed him an arondight blade. He took it, his gaze never leaving Issac's—he was just as 'determined' as Elijah. Another fight was incoming and there was no talking them out of it.

Sighing, I retreated to the wall and leaned against it, crossing my arms over my chest. This wasn't going to end well, but apparently, they had to work it out like 'men'.

When Elijah activated his arondight blade, the Naturals training at the other end of the yard stopped what they were doing and stared. The sword glowed with a dull blue hue. *Interesting.*

Issac brandished his sword and the two clashed. They slashed and countered, spun and flipped, their fight looking more like a dance than two men peacocking over the training yard.

But to my dismay, they were gathering a crowd.

Elijah had proven his point, but the pair wouldn't slowing down for anything. This was becoming more than showing Issac he could fight, and I wished I had a watch so I could check the time.

"Madeleine, there you are," Ramona said, appearing beside me. "I wanted to talk to you about —" She swallowed whatever she was about to say and stared across the yard to where the two men were fighting. "What on earth are they doing now?"

"Measuring the length of their unmentionables," I replied.

"It's a little intense. They look like they're duelling to the death."

"Issac is jealous of Elijah's relationship with me, and Elijah is jealous of Issac's relationship with me." I snorted and rolled my eyes. "Can you keep up?"

Ramona gasped and looked at me. "Am I witnessing a love triangle?"

"Only in their own minds. I made my choice a long time ago."

"Elijah?"

"I doubt I could have freed him from his possession otherwise."

Ramona nodded and turned her attention back to the fight. "So much of the Lady of the Lake's meddling is tied up in love. It's how the Twin Flames could merge and close the rift. It's curious, don't you think?"

"It's more like a foolproof failsafe if you ask me."

"Have I told you how proud I am of you, Madeleine?"

I turned away from Issac and Elijah and frowned. "Proud? Of what?"

"Oh my." She laughed and draped her arm over my shoulders. "From the day you arrived as a frightened seventeen-year-old at the London Sanctum to who you are now… It's like night and day. You've really grown up, Madeleine. Scarlett would be proud."

My heart sank. Ramona's words were meant to cheer me up, but they only reminded me of what was at stake. A rogue Celestial with a death wish was on the loose, and Wilder and Scarlett were still in a coma.

"I better stop those fools before someone gets killed," I said, shrugging her arm off my shoulders.

"Madeleine?"

"We've got work to do," I told her. "I'm not content on waiting for Morgana to come back before we do anything. Would you ask Greer if she could discuss a game plan with me?"

"Can do." She nodded at the fight, which was gathering momentum. "What are you going to do about them?"

I rolled my eyes. "Send them to the naughty corner."

I walked towards the two numbskulls fighting for their so-called honour and allowed my power to simmer.

Their blades flashed as they struck, sending sparks of energy ricochetting across the yard. They locked together, glaring at one another with unmasked dislike.

Seriously. This was so petty.

"*Stop.*" My voice rattled the earth beneath the yard, and everyone fell silent.

Issac and Elijah looked at me, half in shock and the other half still firmly wedged in the danger zone.

"You're acting like children," I hissed. "Issac, you're the vice-Inquisitor or whatever you want to call it. Elijah, you're the last Druid, the wisest people to ever walk this Earth. Get it together. *The both of you.*"

Both men stepped back, allowing their arondight blades to sheath. Luckily for them, they both looked sufficiently sheepish.

"We all get the point," I said. "The entire city *gets the point.* Can we get back to what's important now?"

"Madeleine…" Elijah stepped towards me and I shook my head.

"I'm going to meet Greer," I told them. "Someone has to track down Morgana."

"And it's going to be you?" Issac asked with a frown.

"*Yes.*"

The two men looked at each other, substituting dislike for worry. At least they had *some* good sense.

"This has to be the end of this," I told them. "I can't handle both of you *and* a rogue Celestial."

Everyone had their own problems and insecurities, but they'd mean nothing if we were wiped out of existence. We'd had a game plan against the One. We'd known how to defeat him, but Morgana? There was no instruction manual on how to destroy a celestial being.

Not until someone wrote one, I thought. *Might as well be me.*

Turning my back on Issac and Elijah, I left them to their own devices and went to find Greer.

We had the mother of all takedowns to plan.

7

Greer met me at the remains of the archive.

Morgana's dramatic escape had exposed all four main levels and the destruction was confronting. It was only a small section of the vast tangle of rooms and passageways, but every piece was precious. The courtyard was full of rubble and piles of neatly stacked artefacts. The dig team had sorted ancient books into clear plastic crates to preserve as much as possible before the weather shifted and rain turned all the delicate parchment into mush.

It also looked as if Aiden was trying to take measures to cover the damage to the roof before winter dug its heels in. A temporary structure was being erected—makeshift pylons and pieced together tarpaulins spanned one end of the enormous hole.

"Was there anything else inside the vault?" I wondered out loud.

"Nothing," Greer replied. "It was entirely empty, save for her."

"Well, it would have been awfully dark in there."

"And dull with nothing to do."

I snorted and looked at the wall surrounding the inner bailey of Camelot. It was more like a melted ice sculpture than a formidable defensive structure. Beyond sat the rift, and beside the chasm sat the jagged remains of the castle itself.

This place had taken more than its fair share of beatings and it still stood. Hopefully, it would stand for a few more centuries.

"This was done in less than five minutes," I said. "And I don't think she was even trying."

"If she wanted to destroy us, she would have," Greer admitted. "Morgana wanted to send a message."

"After hundreds of years locked in darkness, it's rather controlled of her, don't you think?"

"A testament to her full capabilities, perhaps."

"Absolute power," I whispered. *How could we fight that?*

"I've summoned everyone," Greer announced. "You're right, Madeleine. We're in over our heads and it's time we think about being proactive."

It was a proper war council, then. I used to bristle about not being included in such discussions, but now it seemed like a burden I wanted no part in. Life was simpler when I was just following orders. There was little responsibility for failure.

It wasn't long before Issac, Aiden, and Thompson joined us. Elijah brought up the rear. He looked confused, as if he didn't understand why he was invited to a meeting with the ultimate hierarchy of Natural-kind. I kind of felt the same way.

"You all understand why we are here," Greer began. "The celestial being, Morgana, has openly declared her hostility on us. I would rather have her on side, to understand who she is and what she desires, but it seems impossible considering her actions towards Madeleine." She glanced at me and I nodded. "Something must be done."

"Like what?" Thomson asked. "Attack, negotiation, defence?"

"A combination of all three," Issac said, "I assume."

"I consulted the Codex, but it wasn't helpful," Greer murmured. "It was strange. I've never…"

"But the Codex is in London," Aiden said. "How…?"

"She's connected to it," Issac explained. "It doesn't matter where it is. The protector always has some measure of contact with its knowledge."

"The mysteries of the Codex," Thompson said with a snort.

"They were meant to remain that way," Greer said. "There are things only the protector is meant to know. However, we are in a new age of our history."

"The Codex doesn't matter," I said with a shake of my head. "Morgana knows everything about us, thanks to me."

"You didn't have a choice," Elijah murmured. "She wanted your memories and there was nothing you or anyone could have done to stop her."

"He's right, Madeleine," Greer said. "No one is to blame for this."

"I would have blamed the Dark," Aiden told us. "But I have a feeling we would've unearthed the archive sooner or later. I'd already found one of the outer walls."

"All this is well and good, but what are we going to do about it?" I asked. "Morgana is coming back. Maybe tomorrow, maybe next week, maybe in a hundred years. Who knows? We have to have some idea of what to do about it."

"We know nothing of the Lady of the Lake or her people," Issac said with a frown. "The archive is unstable, but there are no guarantees we'll find any information on the Celestials. We're talking about a race of creatures who could predate the universe."

"It would take a lifetime to make a dent in that place," Aiden told him. "I doubt we have the time for it anyway."

Everyone looked at Elijah and he shook his head. "Don't look at me. The Druids knew more about the Lady of the Lake than the Naturals, but I was never anyone important."

"Talking to the Druids would be helpful," I said, staring at the archive. "But we need the big guns. We need to find Avalon."

Avalon, otherwise known as Ynys Wydryn—the Isle of Glass.

"Avalon is sealed," Greer said, her eyes widening.

"Then we knock on the door and ask to come in." No one had thought about the Lady of the Lake but me, which meant everyone else thought it was a long shot at best.

"Madeleine, I don't think it's that straightforward," Issac stated. "Avalon is locked in time and space for a reason."

"Avalon was sealed because of the Dark. Wilder and Scarlett defeated the One so there's little risk."

"Until the vault exploded, I would have agreed with you," he argued. "Morgana poses a threat to the Lady, just as she does to us."

"Then we do it covertly." I wasn't giving up so easily. "If Scarlett and Wilder are in a coma because of Morgana's presence, then she likely can't come here for an even greater reason. The only way is to go to her."

"You're awfully fixated on finding Avalon," Aiden commented.

I shot him a look. "Can you think of a better plan?"

"Yeah, as a matter of fact, I do," the archeologist quipped. "We go down into the vault, figure out how she was imprisoned in the first place, and do it again."

I sighed. "Another thing that has a questionable success rate and will take time we don't have."

"And finding a secret pocket of reality in an infinite universe is one hundred percent infallible?"

"At least the Lady of the Lake will know how to defeat Morgana," I stated. Arguing with a nerd was bad business—Aiden had a wider vocabulary than I did.

"Madeleine has a point," Issac said. "The intel would be guaranteed."

"There's still the problem of locating Avalon," Greer mused. "A grain of sand on a beach the size of infinite universes." When she put it like that…I jutted my chin out defiantly. "If we can't find Avalon directly, then we go through the Darklands to the Druid homeland and ask Merlin. He knows the way. He took Scarlett there, remember?"

"You want to go to the Darklands voluntarily?" Thompson asked, his mouth dropping open. "That place is twisted and full of nightmarish creatures. You're crazy."

"Just a little," I said with a smirk.

"Could we contact the Druids?" Greer wondered. "Finding our way through the Darklands is just as difficult as trying to find Avalon."

"Would Merlin even be alive?" Issac asked. "He'd have to be over a thousand years old at least."

Elijah shrugged. "Merlin was old then, even for a Druid."

"How long *does* a Druid live?" Thompson asked, speaking up. He'd been awfully silent up until now.

"It depends," Elijah replied. "But none of this matters without a portal."

"The ones in the archive are gone," Aiden commented, looking into the hole. "You said they only went to places in our world."

"Yes," Elijah said, his shoulders tensing. "We need a Druid and I can't help."

It seemed we'd hit a roadblock.

"The Flames can't exist in the same world as a celestial being," I mused. "Morgana is too powerful to face head-on. Wilder and Scarlett won't wake up until she's gone or dead. We can't put her back in the vault, at least not without a lot of fuss." I looked up at the castle. What I was proposing was dangerous and borderline impossible. "The only way forward I can see, is to find the Lady of the Lake and ask her."

"And the only people who know the way to Avalon, are the Druids," Issac said.

"And we need a portal to get there," Aiden added.

There we're so many impossibilities in my proposal, I was sure Greer would rule in favour of Aiden's idea of reconstructing the vault. Maybe we should try both in case one of us failed.

"What do you know of the Druid homeland, Elijah?" Greer asked, her voice gentle.

"Nothing," he replied, his eyes narrowing. "I never went there."

Greer paced towards the archive and came to a halt at the edge of the hole. She teetered a moment, before turning back to us. "I may know a way."

"A way to Avalon?" Aiden asked, his eyes widening.

"No." She shook her head, her hair cascading around her shoulders. "A way to the Darklands at least."

"It's a start," Issac said, looking hopeful.

"Better than a poke in the eye with a sharp stick," Thompson said, just to say something.

"How?" I asked. If she knew a way past the

boundaries of our world, then things just became interesting indeed.

"Your parents, Madeleine."

I tensed, my breath catching. "My parents?"

"They're researching portal magic," she replied. "When your mother visited last month, she gave me a detailed report on their progress."

"You mean to say my parent's top secret, highly classified project no one is allowed to talk about, is *portals*?" I glanced at Issac, who shrugged. "You knew?"

"I did," he admitted. "But I was unaware they were trying to *open* one."

"Why else would they be researching them?" I huffed.

"Portals use the same structure as the illusion concealing Camelot," Elijah said, sounding impressed. "It would be useful to hide your Sanctum. I hear they're turning that old power station into apartments and shops because that's exactly what the world needs. Less natural resources and more capitalism."

Greer chuckled softly and nodded. "That was the intent of their project, but in light of recent events, their project seems to be our only choice."

I blinked. "So, you agree with me?"

She inclined her head. "We can't hope to face Morgana on our own. She has made it clear she does not want to negotiate. Our best chance lies in Avalon."

"Our only chance," Thompson quipped.

I shook my head in disbelief. Caleb Thompson was agreeing with me? Miracles did happen after all.

"Madeleine and Elijah will meet with the Greenbriars," Greer ordered. "*After* a physical assessment from Ramona."

"And so will I," Issac demanded. "He has no abilities and if Morgana resurfaces—"

"Elijah is a Druid," Greer said. "If anyone goes, it will be him."

"*Great*," the Druid drawled. "I'm looking forward to it."

"And Madeleine is more than capable of withstanding Morgana's presence," the Inquisitor continued. "And I'm sure she will have much to discuss with her parents."

Issac didn't look impressed. "But—"

Greer held up her hand. "The decision has been made."

"Are you sure?" Elijah asked me. "I will go, if that's what you need from me, but the Darklands aren't a walk in the park. The paths are dangerous, and I've never seen them."

"No risk, no reward," I murmured. "If we find your people…"

He smiled. "Don't worry about me, pretty Triune. They can't abandon me a second time thanks to you."

Greer watched us with a curious expression. "Aiden, I would like you to work on rebuilding the vault as a failsafe. We may only get one chance and I'd rather have options in this sea of unknowns."

Aiden nodded enthusiastically. "Of course. I'll get started straight away."

Greer nodded and glanced at each of us. "Dismissed. We have a lot of preparations to make."

"I don't even know why I was here," Thompson said to his brother as they walked towards the thoroughfare.

"I need to get down into the archive," Aiden said. "Can you help me rig some kind of abseiling thing?"

"Abseiling thing?" he scoffed. "Now I know why I'm me, and you're you."

Issac scowled and strode off, annoyed he wasn't coming on our trip to wherever my parents were holed up. I understood his frustration and had some of my own. Greer was trusting Elijah and I to save our people, give or take a species or two. The irony wasn't lost on me.

"Are you sure?" I asked Elijah.

He waited until Greer had moved away before he replied, "I'm not overjoyed, but I don't see any other way. I know as much as you do about Celestials."

"This isn't your fight."

"I may not be a Natural, but I'm a citizen of Camelot," he told me. "Besides, if it's your fight it makes it mine too." He ran his fingers through my hair. "Wherever you go, I follow."

"Even to the Darklands? I hear it's hellish there."

Elijah smiled, though I could feel his nerves lingering just below the surface.

"Even there," he said. "But the Darklands have nothing on meeting your parents."

Elijah and I reported to the infirmary, both our minds heavy with what we were about to attempt. I couldn't even imagine how he was feeling. If we were successful, he would come face-to-face with the people who abandoned him to the Dark.

Seeing my parents—especially my father who hadn't seen me since I'd claimed my Triune soul—seemed like a trifle compared to the things Elijah would have to face.

I sat on the edge of the stainless-steel table Ramona was working at, watching her peer into a microscope. I'd submitted to the physical despite feeling completely fine, and Elijah was going through the motions with Ramona's new assistant at the far end of the room.

"How are you handling all this?" She peered up at me. "You've been through a lot in the last few months, but that encounter with Morgana was…"

I raised an eyebrow. "Next level?"

"That's a good way of describing it."

"I can't seem to die," I told her. "But I'm not keen on testing those limits any time soon."

"*Good.* That's actually what I wanted to talk to you about this morning. Your cell regeneration is a million times more effective than anything I've ever seen. The only people who come close to sharing the same ability are the Twin Flames."

"What does that mean? Will I live forever?"

"You'll age slower, though I'd like to do more study. But…"

"But?"

"Be careful," she murmured. "You were able to prevent your body from dying, but you're not immortal. If your wounds are too great, or if you're struck down in a single blow…" She swallowed hard. "Your body's regeneration can only keep up with so much."

"Understood."

I was kind of glad there was a loophole in the whole immortality thing. Living forever sounded great, but there were at least a thousand drawbacks to being indestructible.

Looking across the infirmary, I watched Elijah as he stretched out his arms and touched each index finger to his nose. He was giving Ramona's new assistant a hard time with his physical, making the poor girl flush.

"Druids live a long time," Ramona said, following my gaze. "But I fear Elijah is more human than Druid right now."

"He'll age faster without his Colours?"

"Yes."

"Does he know?" I asked quietly.

Ramona placed her hand on my arm. "Yes. He understands his reality."

"He never told me," I whispered.

"Knowing Elijah, he probably wanted to save you the worry. There's a lot going on right now."

"Is there any hope?" I asked. "Do you think he can find his way back to his powers?"

"They're there," she replied. "He proved as much when he fought Issac with an arondight blade. As to calling them back, I can't say. His Colours have been dormant a long time, Madeleine. I'm afraid they might not come back at all."

I remembered when he told me that he'd made peace with his lot in life, but it didn't make living with it any easier. I would be devastated if I lost my Light. It was my identity as a Natural, just as it was his as a Druid.

The infirmary door opened and Greer sashayed in. Spotting us at the back, she came over to check on our progress. "All is well, I trust?"

"They both have a perfect bill of health," Ramona replied. "Though I'm not sure Elijah is taking is as seriously as expected."

Greer glanced over her shoulder to where the Druid was joking with the young doctor. "Well, I suppose we need a little comedic relief at a time like this."

"Where are we going exactly?" I asked sliding off the table. "The sooner we can leave, the better."

"Edinburgh," Greer replied.

"Edinburgh?" I raised my eyebrows. "You do know they built the city on a volcano, right? The irony is strong with this one."

"An *extinct* volcano, though I'm sure you'll restrain yourself from filling the streets with lava."

"Do you think we should get your parents a gift?"

Elijah asked, appearing beside Greer. "I want to make a good impression when I meet my girlfriend's makers."

The two women smirked and shared a knowing glance.

"*Light help me*," I moaned.

8

I wasn't exactly thrilled to see my parents, but the tradeoff was the beautiful Scottish capital, Edinburgh.

A city of a thousand lives, it was a hotbed of the historic and modern. From the narrow streets and hidden churchyards of the Old Town, to the Georgian townhouses and latter-day tramway of the New Town.

Bagpipers playing *Scotland the Brave* accompanied Elijah and I as we strolled along the busy Royal Mile —the road that stretched from the ancient Edinburgh Castle at the top of the hill, to the seventeenth century palace of Holyrood at the base. A constant throng of tourists hampered our progress, but despite the dreary weather and bustle, its charm had me by the heart.

It was impossible to cloak ourselves, so we kept our heads down until we'd moved away from the main road. Not that it mattered—no one was paying us any attention.

The grey sky cast a constant drizzle down on the city, forcing human heads under umbrellas and inside hoodies. No one lingered or bothered to look up until they reached the nearest dry zone.

We were bound for the Edinburgh Vaults. They'd been built under the South Bridge in the late seventeenth century as a marvel of engineering at the time. Hidden and closed away underneath the bustling thoroughfare above, they used to house taverns, cobblers, workshops for various other trades, and other shops. As times changed, crime and other unsavoury operations moved in before they'd been sealed off by the authorities. The vaults were forgotten until they'd been reopened in modern times as a curiosity for tourists and ghost hunters.

This was where my parents had hidden their secret portal workshop, right under the noses of tens of thousands of tourists looking for a chilling haunted encounter. I wondered how many sightings of the paranormal had been caused by their Natural shenanigans.

I could scarcely wrap my brain around how the city crowded around the bridge. It ran together to the point you'd be forgiven if you forgot there was another layer of Edinburgh beneath, alive with vibrant shops and pubs.

"Parking is so expensive here," Elijah grumbled as we moved away from the Royal Mile. "It's daylight robbery!"

"Greer gave me some money and a credit card," I told him. "Don't worry about it."

"I can't believe someone gave you an expense account."

"I can't believe someone gave you a sword."

"I know and it *feels good*." To his delight, Elijah had been given his own arondight blade *and* a cold iron dagger. Hopefully we wouldn't have to use them, but all bets were off.

We turned into an alleyway—they were called closes in this part of the city—and made our way along the dark and narrow passage. The buildings were so tall here, no sunlight reached the bottom, no matter what time of day it was. A chill hung in the air and moisture dripped down the stone walls on either side.

The deeper we ventured amongst the echoes of Edinburgh's Old Town, the more connected to the spirit world I felt. I didn't know what it was about this place, but it felt as if I was being watched by an unknown force.

"Did you know the Dark loved to hang out here in the Middle Ages?" Elijah stated. "If this was the seventeenth century, we'd be wading through human waste and disease. Demons loved that stuff."

"You really know how to romance a woman," I drawled.

"The castle was only a few decades old when I was born," he went on. "But people lived there since the Bronze Age."

"They were really smart, living on top of a volcano."

"It became extinct a few hundred million years ago. Besides, I don't think the people understood what it was. They built here because of the elevation. They could see for miles from the castle. It's an imposing defensive position."

"The high ground always is." I paused at the end of the close and looked up at him. "You're talking a lot. Are you nervous?"

"Of course, I'm nervous," he huffed. "I'm meeting your parents, who you never speak about, and I don't have a gift to give them. You wouldn't let me stop for a box of chocolates and now I'm shamed."

"They don't care for sweets," I told him, "or gifts."

I knew my mother had preconceived notions about Elijah, but that was before he'd been cured. She warned me away the last time we'd spoken about him. It would be an uphill battle for him to earn her respect and no box of chocolates would help bridge the gap. Then there was my father, who usually went along with her to avoid arguments.

"Naturals are so picky," Elijah quipped. "Maybe I should have brought them something sharp and stabby. I know how they like their weapons."

"I appreciate the thought, Elijah, but my parents are more impressed by actions. We were never a close-knit family. I was at the Academy for most of my life while they were off on their secret missions. Love came in a letter with an exotic stamp when I got good grades.”

“I see,” he said thoughtfully. “I know the type.”

I hesitated. “Were your parents the same?”

“A Druid is only as good as the complexity of their prisms.”

“Well, my parents can be…old-fashioned.”

“Is that code for something?”

“You know it is.”

I leaned against the wall and looked down the street. We were alone. The weather was too miserable for much foot traffic outside of the main tourist areas.

“I understand,” Elijah said. “They have preconceived notions about my former life.”

“I wouldn’t worry. They have preconceived notions about me and I’m their daughter.”

“I wish we’d had more time to talk about these things,” he murmured.

“Me too.”

He smiled at me, his gaze studying my features. Whatever he thought about the imminent meeting, he kept to himself. “So, where is this secret lair?”

“It’s a workshop,” I replied, thankful we didn’t have to hash out our parental issues on the street. “And it’s along here someplace. There’s a ward concealing the entrance.”

I let go of my powers and allowed a trickle to permeate the surrounding air. Leading the way down the narrow street, I scanned the entrances to pubs and bars, looking for the way to the workshop.

Ahead, a cobalt blue door shimmered out of the wall like a mirage.

"There," I said.

"Nice magic trick," Elijah said.

"You can see it?"

"I can see through your wards and sense lingering power just fine," he replied. "It's the other bits that are out of my reach."

I slipped my hand into his and squeezed. "Any last words?"

"I'm sure it's not that dire."

I thought of my parents as I knocked on the door. Elijah was nervous, I could feel him squirming behind me, but so was I.

I was my mother's daughter in looks—we were both willowy, ivory-skinned, and black-haired—and in temperament, which was probably why we butted heads more often than not. She was quick to anger and so was I. We both excelled at combat and strategic planning. Theory and book smarts were tedious affairs, but doable.

My father, on the other hand, was another creature entirely.

He was impossibly tall, blond, and studious. Though he loved his books and scientific notions towards Light, people had often made the mistake of underestimating his brute strength and skill with a blade. All Naturals were trained in combat—at least in part—and my father had turned out to be one of those annoying people who was good at everything they picked up. Not the kind of talented that excelled him to godlike status, but the kind where he was good enough to breeze through life. I liked to think it was adaptability more than anything.

He was the one to open the door and the sight of him was strange, yet familiar. I hadn't seen him in a few years, and I was lost for what to say.

"Madeleine!" He stood back to let us pass and eyed Elijah as we entered the workshop.

"Hey, Dad," I said as I looked around the vault, which turned out to be much larger than I'd anticipated.

The roof was curved, which was where the vaults had gotten their name—from the vaulted ceiling—and completely made of old bluestone blocks. They had set a living area up in one end, with a couch, coffee table, rug, and small kitchenette.

At the rear of the vault was the workshop itself. The walls were covered in coloured Post-It notes and other bits of paper. A whiteboard with scrawled equations was dragged to the edge of a table where empty coffee cups and a half-eaten sandwich lay forgotten. They had cleared a space in the centre of the room and I frowned at the scorch marks on the stone.

It was like Greer had said—they were trying to open a portal. I could smell the metallic tang mix with the damp earthen stench of the enclosed vault.

I shucked off my jacket and draped it across the back of the couch. It was warm inside for such a chilled hole in the wall.

"Madeleine?" My mother poked her head out of yet another room at the back. "Is that you?"

Elijah moved closer to me as she came to join us.

"This is my mother, Bethany Greenbriar," I said. "And that is my father, Edward."

"And who do we have here?" Dad looked him over with a critical eye.

"This is Elijah. He's a Druid."

My parents hesitated for a moment.

"A Druid?" Dad asked. "How is that possible?"

Elijah worried his bottom lip and raised his eyebrows at me.

"How can you be a Druid when the last time I heard, you were a demon," Mum declared. She glared at me, clearly disappointed in my poor judgment. *How dare I smear the good name of Greenbriar.* "What's going on here, Madeleine? I warned you about letting him into your life, yet here he stands."

"He's not a demon," I cried. "Use your Light, and you'll see I'm telling you the truth. Elijah is a Druid."

"That's what everyone keeps telling me," Elijah drawled.

"Clearly Greer only gave you the cliff notes version," I seethed, my hands shaking. My anger was rising and so was my power. "It's a wonder she even told you about Morgana."

"It may be as you say," Mum argued, "but it doesn't erase the things he's done."

"It was you who told me that it doesn't matter what you are, *only who you choose to be*," I snarled. "I freed his soul from Ikakantor. There is no Darkness in him anymore. He could have left and turned his back on us the moment Morgana broke out of the vault, but he's here."

"Well, this escalated fast," Elijah muttered to himself.

"You're half Dark," Dad said. "But you were born Natural. No daughter of mine will associate with a demon."

Elijah snorted. "Technically, she's one third Dark."

"What I am is a Triune," I declared. "Light, Dark, and *Druid*." Mum fell silent and shook her head in disbelief. "And what you are, are hypocrites. Elijah was born a Druid, just as I was born a Natural."

Mum blinked and glanced at Elijah. "I thought…"

"I know what you thought," I hissed. "You thought that lava I raised was demonic. Well, as it turns out, it wasn't."

"We didn't know, Madeleine," Dad said. "We thought—"

"You would know if you weren't so focused on your work and blind to your only child!"

They fell silent and the already icy workshop turned arctic and I fancied I could almost hear the noise of the city above.

Elijah squirmed beside me. "Well, this is uncomfortable."

"It's a long story," I said to fill the gap and buy some time. It was a whole other can of demons I didn't want to open.

"How old are you?" Dad asked, narrowing his eyes at Elijah. At least he was making an effort, no matter how blunt.

"Eight hundred and forty-nine," the Druid declared.

Mum choked on her own spit and I smirked.

"Technically, Camelot fell eight hundred and twenty-three years ago," he went on. "I was twenty-six at the time, so…"

"You were at the fall of Camelot?" Mum asked, her curiosity winning over her prejudice. "Really?"

Elijah squirmed. "Erm…"

It was a time he hadn't even spoken to me about, so I butted in before it became any more uncomfortable.

"I thought we'd worked this out when I saw you at Camelot, Mum, but clearly not. It doesn't matter. We're here under orders from the Regula." I shifted into solider-mode. It was a tone they'd responded well to after all. "Time is short. I gather Greer has spoken to you about what happened at Camelot?"

"Yes," Dad replied, turning his attention onto me. "We heard from her last night."

"A celestial being, locked underneath Camelot," Mum began with an awed expression. "It's unfathomable!"

"And one hundred percent real." I shook my head. "I witnessed her power and whatever she does next won't be pretty."

"Celestial beings have the potential to create worlds," Elijah stated. If he was hurt by the way they'd treated him so far, he wasn't showing it. He had more strength and tact than I did, all things considered. I was a little jealous.

I coughed and curled my fingers into tight fists. "Which means if she was angry enough, she would wipe the entire planet out with no effort whatsoever."

"That's why you want to find the Lady of the Lake," Dad murmured.

I nodded. "She's our only hope, but to find Avalon, we have to find the Druids."

"Apparently, we have one standing right here," Mum said, looking over Elijah with her trademark critical glare. Clearly, she still didn't believe us.

"I don't have my Colours, but I know a thing or two about portals," Elijah told them. "Perhaps I can help with your project?"

Dad snorted and Mum shooshed him.

"Colours?" she asked.

"We have Light, they have Colours," I replied.

"That we can weave into prisms," Elijah added. "It's like a spirograph, but much cooler."

Tense silence followed his good-natured joke and I couldn't help the pang of disappointment that hit me right in the heart. I wanted them to like him, I just wasn't aware how much until I was standing here.

Mum turned her gaze onto me. "Madeleine, can I speak to you…in private?"

She curled her hand around my wrist and dragged me to the opposite end of the workshop, casting a cloak of silence around us. I glanced over my shoulder at Elijah, who was staring after us with a pained expression. He was disappointed, too. He'd wanted to make a good impression so badly.

"I was expecting to see Issac," she said, glowering at me. *And there it was.* Issac was obviously the better choice for me.

After visiting Camelot and fawning all over the guy, Mum was probably already planning our summer wedding and dreaming of all her *Natural* grandchildren. I wouldn't be surprised if there was a mood board full of flower arrangements, wedding dresses, and meal plans on the other side of that whiteboard.

"Sorry to disappoint you," I drawled, "but I didn't want you to feel left out of the pity party." *And I didn't want children.*

"This mission is too important, Madeleine. We need our best people on this. Not a powerless Druid." She'd stood there probing his abilities beyond a surface detection, *without his consent*, the whole time we'd been talking. *Typical.*

"I came here hoping for a warm welcome and a hug or two, not a cross examination." I swallowed the lump in my throat and squashed down my simmering power. "He wanted to bring you a gift, for Light's sake, and all you can do is look at him like he's a monster."

"He was a demon for centuries," she argued. "How can he be the man he was before after that long? He can't, Madeleine. The Dark may be gone, but it's shaped his mind. He could turn on you!"

"You don't know him."

"He's not good for you."

"*Stop*. I'm a grown woman," I hissed, "I can make my own decisions."

She grabbed my arm. "*Madeleine*."

"I don't care, Mum," I said, wrenching out of her grasp. "Elijah and I are a package deal. We need each other beyond this mission."

"Do you love him?"

"I don't know." I shrugged and shook my head. "I'm still trying to come to terms with what I've become, but what I do know is that Elijah is a good man who's suffered more heartbreak and pain than any person should. He walked this world for eight hundred years looking for salvation until chance brought us together. I was made Triune by mistake, but it was that one tiny split-second that made all the difference to him. If I hadn't become my family's greatest shame, he would never have found his freedom. I will not abandon him just because you and Dad disapprove."

"*Madeleine Greenbriar*." Her cheeks were reddening, and I wasn't sure if it was because of embarrassment or anger. Perhaps if we were closer, I'd be able to tell the difference.

"I've faced a great deal of prejudice for something that was out of my control, but I never expected to get it from my own parents." I wondered why I was so disappointed. When we'd last spoken at Camelot, I thought she'd come to terms with my unfortunate lot in life, but here we were having the same argument, only this time Elijah had been dragged into it. "I'm not looking for your blessing or your forgiveness. All I want is your portal."

Her expression darkened and her lips thinned. She was mad, then.

"Fine," she said. "The mission is the priority."

She walked away and rejoined the others, our fragile relationship teetering on the edge.

It was then that I realised why I felt so empty inside. My parents had broken my heart. Saying they loved me was one thing, but actually feeling it was another.

All I'd ever wanted was to belong, but I couldn't even seem to fit in with my own parents. I was a constant disappointment. Bringing Elijah here was a mistake, but we needed a portal.

Did all this mean anything in the grand scheme of a celestial being destroying everything in her path? Probably not, but it still hurt.

Sighing, I sat on the couch and gathered my courage. I had a feeling I was going to need every scrap I could find.

9

The air smelt like damp and dirt, with a tinge of old rotten boots.

I lingered at the far end of the workshop, watching my parents reluctantly go over the premise of their portal research with Elijah.

From the way my parents threw themselves into their work, I'd always wondered if I was an accident. This didn't seem like a healthy environment to bring a child into the world on purpose. Maybe I should ask, but now didn't seem like the time. Actually, asking would make another kind of volcano erupt. Best to leave that box tightly shut.

I was sitting on the worn couch, leafing through a human newspaper when Dad approached. Humans sure whined about the strangest things, but I guess we all had our buttons.

"Is opening a portal workable?" I asked, tossing the paper aside.

His expression closed off and he nodded. "We

have had some success. Elijah has already put forth some elements we never considered. With some recalibration, we just might find the Darklands."

"Good." I didn't like to linger when danger was looming. I was a woman of action and seeing my parents had only stoked the fire of getting out of here.

"Are you sure you want to go?" he asked. "Without his powers, Elijah is just a man."

"The Druids will help him get them back," I said thinly. "Until then, he has me."

"A Triune," he mused. "It's a curious thing, Madeleine."

I felt the weight of my cold iron dagger in my boot. "Curious or loathsome?"

"I didn't say that."

"I'm part demon, Dad. I can't forget the way people treated me when it was all *they* thought I was. Even when I was 'cured,' the cruelty never went away." I glanced across the workshop. "I saw the way you looked at Elijah. It's the same way people used to look at me."

"Sweetheart, you were Dark for barely a year."

"Seven and a half months," I corrected.

He sighed. "Elijah was bound for over eight hundred years."

"It doesn't excuse the way you and Mum spoke to him," I hissed. "There are shades of grey in this world, Dad. It's not all Light and Dark." I rose to my feet, my head beginning to throb. My power was bubbling, reacting to my emotions. "Elijah is a Druid. *Just* a Druid. His knowledge and good heart are what's going to help us face Morgana. Enough with the victim shaming."

"*Madeleine.*"

I strode towards the door.

"Madeleine, where are you going?" he demanded.

"For a walk," I snapped. "It's suffocating in here."

<hr>

Outside, the rain had stopped.

The sun was already dipping low towards the horizon. The days were becoming shorter the closer the depths of winter came, even more so in Scotland.

I buried into my jacket and allowed a cloak of invisibility to settle over me. Concealed from human eyes, I walked with no destination in mind.

So much had happened since the first day I set foot in Camelot. I'd changed irrevocably and faced so many unknowns, I wasn't sure which way was up anymore. I certainly wasn't expecting what had just happened with my own family.

I emerged from the lane beside South Bridge and stepped onto the Royal Mile. It was heaving with crowds taking advantage of the lull in the inclement weather. A bagpiper dressed in a white shirt, kilt, matching sash, and tailored coat was on the corner playing a shrill song. A group of people assembled for a walking tour by the mercat cross—the market cross in old Scots. It was a small monument where markets were held, proclamations were made, and where people were executed in the 'olden days'.

I crossed the Mile and wove a path past the gaudy souvenir shops and ducked into a small opening amongst the bustle.

It really was a pretty place, full of romance, mystery, and mayhem. I kind of wished Elijah and I could have come here under better circumstances. We could have walked the streets arm in arm, lingered in one of the warm pubs, explored the hidden nooks and crannies, climbed the wild crags of Arthur's Seat, and had a real romantic getaway. We hadn't had any time…for anything really.

I was strolling down a long stairway within one of Edinburgh's famous closes when I sensed the familiar buzz of Darkness in the air—a demon lurked somewhere close.

I hadn't hunted in months. Not since last summer when I'd first met Elijah. I kind of missed it in a twisted way. The thrill of the chase had always been an intoxicating lure for me, even more so when I was on my own.

Glancing down the stairs, my power sizzled as I detected the creature lurking inside a human male who was walking towards me. He hadn't seen me yet, or if he had, he pretended not to notice me. I was cloaked, but it didn't matter to the Dark. It was humans I was concealed from, not putrid parasitic shite stains.

I continued down the stairs, aware of the approaching threat. I had more power at my disposal this time, but I wasn't sure how it translated to demon hunting. Not yet.

Reaching out with my power, I brushed against the creature ever so slightly.

It was an Infernal. Its natural form was a cloud of Darkness, much like that of a greater demon, but much less powerful. They loved to hop between human bodies, possessing and causing as much trouble as they could. Infernals were vulgar and violent at best and held onto their host at all costs. A full exorcism had to be performed to even loosen it from its body of choice.

I hadn't seen one in years. We'd thought they'd mostly evaporated after the rift was closed, though a few of the strongest had clung to life just long enough to be exorcised and destroyed by Natural patrols. The only demons we'd faced these days were the cockroaches of Darkness—greater demons, the ex-residents of Camelot who'd managed to keep their original forms, and small-time demonic essences who were so insignificant, they didn't even have a designated name. But those were just the ones we knew about.

I might be looking at the last of a parasitic subspecies. That's why I couldn't let it walk away.

I narrowed my eyes at the man, who smirked at me, finally revealing he was aware of my presence. It was going to put up a fight and I had to be quick if I was going to save the innocent it was currently hitching a ride inside.

I reached for my power, focusing my intent on exorcising the demon, and froze.

An ethereal hand reached towards the man and it

took a moment for me to realise it was my own. My essence peeled away from my physical body, forging through a place of timelessness.

The world slowed down around me as I moved towards the possessed man. Pedestrians hovered mid-stride on the steep stairs. Cars and busses came to a halt on the road below. Pigeons hovered in the sky. Even the demon seemed to be frozen.

My ghostly hand passed through the human and grasped the Darkness within. Not understanding what I was doing, I pulled. The Infernal tore out of the man with an awful sucking sound and began to spark angrily.

I clung to it, squashing the inky cloud in my palm. Strange. It had substance here.

The Infernal began to hiss and spit before it broke apart. Blobs of black slime hit the footpath, dissolving like droplets of water on a hot surface.

I watched the last of it disappear and shook my head in disbelief. Had I just killed it? I looked up at the man who hadn't moved a muscle. He seemed fine, but who knew how he'd react once I stepped back into my own body.

Flame flared in front of me and Morgana appeared like a bolt of lightning, striking the ground. The force of her landing buffeted me back a step and I held onto my panic.

How did she know I was here? If she found out what we were trying to do, the battle would be over before it had a chance to begin.

"These creatures are so dull," the Celestial said,

walking around the man I'd just pulled the Infernal from. "Their brains are so small they can't even see what's happening to their world."

"Humans deserve to be left in peace."

"Oh, darling, tell the truth for once in your life. Humans do not understand our kind, that's why you keep your existence secret from them. Once, they would have revered you like gods, but it's too late to reveal yourselves—they've grown too much. If you stepped out of the shadows, they would brand you a monster and they'd kill you on the spot." She swept her arm across the vista and sneered, "These are the creatures you've vowed to protect? They don't deserve it."

"Oh, and I bet you're about to tell me what they deserve instead."

"*Darkness.*"

"That's where you've got it wrong, Morgana," I snarled. "We protect this world and everything on it. It's not just for humanity. It's for *life.*"

"Is that what she told you when she gave you her power? We don't protect life, we create it and *we take it away*. That's what gods do."

"Who? The Lady of the Lake?"

"I can't believe you worship that snivelling child," she hissed. "You should worship *me.*"

"It's not about worship." I shook my head, knowing I was poking an unstable beehive.

"You'll see, *abomination*. After I've had my revenge on the Naturals, I will wipe this world clean." She raised her arms, her exposed skin ripping with crimson fire. "I will purge it with fire and rebuild it anew. *Shadow and flame will rule.*"

Morgana rushed at me, pushing my ethereal form back into my body. I gasped as the world sped up and cried out as her hand wrapped around my throat. Before I could counterstrike, she lifted me up into the air and carried me up and away from the city.

She was mad. All those years stuck in the vault must have eroded her sanity. There was no rhyme or reason behind her actions. One moment she was angry, the next she was jealous, then she wanted to be worshipped. I couldn't keep up.

The one thing I did know was an unstable Celestial was even bigger bad news than a sane one.

Cold air rushed past my face as Morgana's touch burned around my neck. I was trapped in her grasp, the Earth far below. I knew I could do some incredible things, but flying was not one of them. There was nothing I could do to stop her.

The world spun as Morgana flew, holding me in her clutches like a predatory bird. I was reminded of Scarlett's story about the Druidess Gilhana shapeshifting into a hawk, but I knew this tale wasn't going to have quite the same ending.

The Celestial let me go and I fell, twisting and turning in the air. I landed awkwardly, my boots hitting rocky earth so hard I fell onto my knees. Pain vibrated through my legs and throbbed around my neck, but I looked up.

We were on the pinnacle of Arthur's Seat. Edinburgh stretched below, the earthy toned buildings merged with the brilliant green of the Scottish landscape. The castle stood tall amongst all the hubbub, an ancient beacon shining brighter than the modern. Here and there, streetlights had begun to turn on in the lengthening shadows of twilight.

Morgana stood a few paces away, staring at me like I was a pile of something nasty stuck to her shoe.

"What do you call yourself? Madeleine?" She sneered down at me. "You are quite pretty for such a pathetic thing. Druid, Natural, and Dark. How much do you know, I wonder?"

"*Enough.*" My knees dug into the rocky ground and I began to shiver as my power rushed to heal the burns on my neck.

"I doubt it." The Celestial sighed and raised her hands. "Shall we see?"

The ground began to tremble and my heartbeat quickened. What the hell was she doing?

She tilted her head to the side. "Can you feel that? Can you feel the Earth stir?"

I pressed my palms on the ground and felt the vibrations. One word flashed in my mind and it wasn't good. *Fire.*

Fire, brimstone, inferno, magma, lava, *death.*

Morgana was awakening the volcano underneath Edinburgh. *Shite...*

"Enough!" I shouted. "I get that you're powerful. There's no need to murder innocent humans to prove your point."

Her eyes sparkled with a cosmos of stars. "Who said anything about murder?"

I realised she was testing me, but why? Morgana had made it clear she thought I was a monster fit for extermination, so why the about face? She must have found a use for me…

I pushed to my feet, centring myself on the rolling earth. *I was no one's puppet.*

"I won't let you do this. I won't allow it." My own kind of fire awakened in me, stirred by the anger the Celestial had sparked. "This isn't your world to toy with, Morgana."

I swallowed my panic as I realised I was about to attempt to quieten a restless volcano.

Be calm, Madeleine. Be calm and think.

My emotions were linked to my abilities. Issac had helped me tame them so I wouldn't lose control, but now wasn't the time for restraint. It was the time to show this bitch how we did things in our reality. So…

I let go.

Power leeched out of me, travelling through the earth like tree roots searching for water. Darkness, Colours, and Light merged into one, glowing so bright I felt like I was becoming a star myself.

Awareness spread through me, pulling my mind into the Earth where the flame Morgana had stirred was forging a path through the iron crust that shielded the surface of the planet from its molten core.

Liquid fire was racing towards the summit of the caldera underneath Edinburgh, threatening to explode and shatter the city below. Half a million people lived in the tightly wound streets and countryside. If I couldn't force the volcano to still…

My parents were down there. My parents and Elijah.

I screamed as the ground splintered, radiating outwards like a multitude of lightning bolts. The rotting stench of brimstone filled the air as the gas hissed from the fissures, but I held on, pushing the lava down with every shred of essence I could pull from my soul.

The lava ground to a halt, the pressure building until I thought I was the one who was going to do the exploding. My throat was raw as I pushed against the untamed forces of the planet, crying out as searing pain tore through my body.

Slowly, but surely, the boiling lava began to calm to a simmer, then bubble back towards the Earth's core.

When my power cut out, I collapsed. I lay on the broken earth and breathed heavily, staring at the sky.

Morgana was nowhere to be found. I didn't know when she'd left, but it hardly seemed to matter.

Move, Madeleine. Move.

A spark of Light pulsed in my heart and I rolled onto my side. I was on my feet, propelled by the dull string of energy. I made it down from Arthur's Seat and onto the road beside the Palace of Holyroodhouse, completely in a daze.

The city was in an uproar. Sirens wailed and people milled around in a state of shock, taking photos and videos of the chaos on their smartphones. I barely registered them as I dragged myself along the Royal Mile, and they never saw my weary passage.

Light help me…

The walls of the narrow close beside South Bridge closed in on me. My vision began to slip.

I'd used too much power.

Finally, I crashed through the door of the workshop, vaguely aware my parents were arguing. When I appeared, everything fell silent and I stumbled across the room. I was fading.

Mum's hand flew to her mouth. "Madeleine, your eyes…"

"*Morgana*," I rasped, ignoring her. "She's here. She's—"

I stumbled, Elijah caught me, and then there was nothing. Nothing at all.

10

————

Fevered images flashed through my mind.

Visions of the past, present, and future intertwined as I floated in unconsciousness. Were the creatures who inhabited my soul trying to tell me something? Was it the demon Eilhana and the unknown Druid who made up my Triune calling out in the darkness?

There was no way of knowing.

I'd wake and forget all of this. I already was.

The dreams slipped through my fingers like water and I took a deep breath.

My eyes opened.

I stared at the vaulted ceiling and listened to the raised voices in the next room. My parents were arguing. *Loudly.*

The bed I was laying in was soft, the mattress moulding around my body like soft butter. *Memory foam.* I didn't know why that was important, but it was something real I could focus on while my faculties evened out.

"It's all over the news," my mother said. "This is too big for us to conceal. What if she does it again?"

"If she didn't do something, Morgana would have done worse," Elijah said.

"How do we know it was Morgana?" Mum said. "Madeleine can control lava. I saw it with my own eyes at Camelot."

I sat up and rubbed my temples, the blanket falling away. My parents thought I was the problem? *Typical.*

I felt my anger rise again and I took a deep breath, using the exercises Issac had taught me. Oxygen filled my lungs and I held steady for a beat, then let it all out in one long slow exhale.

"She's the only one of her kind. No one understands what she's capable of," Dad said, "not even Madeleine."

"She's proven herself time and time again," Elijah declared. "I don't know how many times she has to in order for you to see her as the same person she's always been."

"And you knew her before?" Mum demanded. "Have you been watching our daughter?"

"No!" Elijah scoffed, and I could picture his handsome face contorting with frustration. "I met her before her soul changed."

"*Stay away from her.*"

"Oh, now you want to protect her?" the Druid demanded. "This whole time you've been treating her like she's a problem that needs solving, not embracing her for who she is—*your daughter*, who is the most loyal, caring, and determined person I've ever known. The Light in her is beyond compare."

I gritted my teeth and clambered out of bed, unable to take it anymore. It was difficult enough trying to control what I'd become, let alone listen to the bickering that was going on in the next room.

The stone floor was cold and the chill spread through my bare feet as I strode to the door. Shoving it open, it swung around and slammed into the wall with a dull bang.

"*Enough.*"

Everyone turned to stare at me, and my parents at least had the good grace to look embarrassed. My mother's cheeks flushed red and Dad glanced at the floor.

"I can't believe you," I hissed. "I used all of my power to stop the volcano, not wake it." I leaned against the doorjamb, shaking. "I saw an Infernal in the street and I excised it. Morgana must have been waiting for me to reveal myself and decided to go all crazy again. *She was testing me.*" I shook my head, my hair falling forwards like a black curtain. "I can't believe I'm standing here defending myself to my own parents. *Again.*"

Mum took a hesitant step forwards. "Madeleine."

"*Don't.*" I narrowed my eyes in warning. "I need you both more than I ever have in my entire life. I need my mum and dad. How can you stand there and only see a freak of nature and not me? *I'm Madeleine.*"

"Darling, you're not a freak," Dad began, but I held up my hand.

"Your words and actions don't match, so don't be surprised when I say I don't believe you."

Elijah moved beside me and rubbed his palm along my arm. "You're cold," he murmured.

"I used all of my power," I told him. "That's why."

"Madeleine saved the city," he said to my parents, his voice taking on a cool tone I hadn't heard before. "And I doubt Morgana will be happy about it. We need to open the portal as soon as possible."

Mum's lips thinned and Dad nodded. "We'll work on it." He glanced at me. "Sweetheart?"

I met his gaze, unsure.

"Get some rest," he told me. "You're going to need your strength in the Darklands."

* * *

I sat on the bed and dragged the blanket around me. My power was slowly regenerating, its metallic threads winding along my veins, entwining with my nerve endings, warming me as it went.

I stared at the closed door, knowing my parents were on the other side working on the portal.

"I'm just disappointed," I murmured as Elijah perched next to me. "They jumped to the worst conclusion without even speaking to me first. If they'd just asked…" I sighed and lowered my gaze. "They'll never understand."

"This was what they grew up with." Elijah took a deep breath and smoothed my hair back. "We're asking them to change their entire belief system. The war between the Light and Dark is all they've ever known. Give them some time."

"How are you so calm right now?"

"I'm tempted to revert to Dark Elijah to fight for your honour, don't you worry about that." His expression faded into something a bit more gentle. "Tell me what happened."

I settled against the pillows, hoping the South Bridge and my parents' wards were strong enough to shield us from Morgana. She was still out there, likely angry that I passed her test. I'd saved Edinburgh but revealed myself as a threat. Now I was a target and the Darklands were the only place I could go to avoid facing the Celestial again. Luckily, that's exactly where we needed to be.

I told Elijah everything that had happened after I'd left the workshop up until the point I'd stood on top of Arthur's Seat and calmed the volcano. "I think Morgana's mind is eroding. She was even more erratic than she was at Camelot."

Elijah was lost in thought for a moment. "Maybe that's why she was in the vault to begin with."

"It had to have been Arthur and the Naturals of Camelot who put her there in the first place. Maybe even the Druids helped."

"If it was, it was before I was born. Besides, a threat like that wouldn't have been made public."

I thought about all the things we knew about

Morgana—which weren't many—and began to piece together a theory. Scarlett had told me that they couldn't exist in the same time and space as her. That was a huge clue.

Had the Lady of the Lake imprisoned Morgana so she could claim our world for her own? It didn't feel right. The Lady was a pure and good Celestial. Why would she give the Naturals her power and create the Twin Flames if she wasn't? It had to be because she was protecting us, just as she had with the Dark.

All that was certain was that we had to find her as soon as possible. Morgana had already made it clear she could reignite extinct volcanos without breaking a sweat. I'd called forth the same kind of flame, but now I understood it took a lot more grunt to turn an entire planet into a smoking pit of hellfire. I didn't have it in me, but Morgana? Morgana could remake entire *universes*.

"When I excised the Infernal, I wonder…" I began. "Well, I kind of *stepped* out of my body. I was essence."

Elijah didn't seem surprised. "Druids can manipulate time and space by folding pockets of time into illusions, but it isn't just parallel universes and portals. The spiritual world is just another layer of reality."

"Are you saying you can speak to the dead?"

He shrugged. "Not exactly. I knew of some Druids who could, but they were much older and more powerful. It's a rare ability, but the spiritual world exists and can be contacted. Some humans have the same skill, you know. Majorly diluted, though."

"Is there anything Druids can't do?" I sighed. The more I heard about them, the more I wondered if the Druids were a little overpowered.

"We can do many things, but not all of them," he explained. "Druids are linked to the elements and the forces that bind them."

"So, you have specialities?"

"Something like that."

"I better not be ridiculously overpowered because I won't be able to handle the pretentiousness of it all. It's bad enough being an unstable Triune."

"Perfection is overrated," Elijah chuckled. "We can do a little of everything, but fire seems to be your thing."

"What was yours?"

His smile faded and I began to regret asking, so I kissed him instead. His touch was quick to deepen and I shivered, but it wasn't from the cold. I was warm through and through.

"*Madeleine*," he whispered as he pulled away.

The depth of his feelings terrified me, and I was becoming more and more anxious I was going to hurt him. Elijah had centuries of understanding and I barely knew anything. My inexperience was going to drive him away sooner or later, I was sure of it. Perhaps that's why I was so reluctant to let go and cross the final line of intimacy with him.

"I'm feeling much better," I said. "I'm all

recharged."

He smiled. "I—"

Whatever he was going to say was broken off as the door opened and Mum appeared holding a mobile phone. She coughed nervously, embarrassed by our closeness.

She glanced at Elijah, then held out the phone towards me. "It's Greer. She'd like to speak with you."

Elijah rose, saving me the trouble of leaving the bed and thanked her. I didn't think she deserved his politeness, but I was still angry at her. He handed me the phone and I narrowed my eyes.

"I'll leave you to it," she muttered, taking the hint.

When she'd closed the door behind her, I pressed the phone to my ear. "Greer?"

"Madeleine," came the protector's worried voice. "Are you all right?"

Disclosure was something I'd recklessly risked the night I'd met Elijah at that nightclub in London. This time, it was even worse.

"I couldn't help it," I blurted. "If I didn't do something, the whole area would be a smoking ruin. There was no way to avoid it."

"I understand."

I hesitated. "You do?"

"Madeleine, you were up against a Celestial," she replied. "This was the best outcome we could have hoped for under the circumstances. The human media is reporting it as an earthquake, nothing more."

"In a region of the world that isn't supposed to get

them."

"Take the win, Madeleine," Greer said with a soft laugh. "The Regula certainly is."

"The human media will have something else to talk about other than political economics for a change," Elijah quipped. "You've provided stable employment for seismologists around the globe."

I groaned. "When you put it like that…"

"Your parents assure me the portal is nearing completion," Greer said on the other end of the phone. "This may be the last opportunity I have to speak with you before you leave."

"Any last wishes?"

"You know the mission," she replied. "Aiden is working on the vault, but our hopes lay with you and Elijah finding the Lady of the Lake."

"I know." The heavy weight of reality pressed down on my shoulders. We might be all that stood between Morgana and the end of the world.

"I believe in you, Madeleine," Greer said. "You and Elijah."

My heart leapt and I felt tears burn my eyes as my throat tightened. They were the very words I'd wanted to hear from my mum and dad.

At that moment, I missed Scarlett and Wilder more than I ever had. They'd become my surrogate parents in a way, and now so had Greer. I wondered if she realised that's how I felt.

Elijah rested his palm on my knee and squeezed.

"Thank you," I managed to choke out. "I won't let you down."

11

My power had fully returned by the next morning.

I sat at the table in the workshop, suffering through an awkward breakfast with my father and Elijah while my mother was in the shower. We'd been here long enough for my untouched toast to go stone cold, so I knew she was avoiding me. I couldn't blame her—I'd do the same thing if I wasn't stuck in a vault underneath a centuries' old bridge.

I picked up the newspaper, swiped my thumb over the black type, and read the headline. *Earthquake Chaos - Edinburgh Shaken to its Core.*

"This is taking too long," I complained, scowling at the ink on my finger.

"Portals take time, especially when we're trying to conjure one up from nothing," Dad said, peering at me over his coffee. Why he needed to drink the stuff was beyond me. A touch of Light and he'd be wide awake. "I don't want to accidentally send my only daughter into nothingness. Sending her to the Darklands are bad enough."

I snorted, thinking he wouldn't mind blasting me off into outer space given half the chance, and turned my attention back to the newspaper.

"The difference between our generations is staggering, Madeleine," he told me. *"We're trying."*

Silence fell in the vault and it was so absolute, I could hear my father's heartbeat. The stone was so thick it masked the noise from the bustling city above, so I was sure the rhythm I heard was well within the cardio region.

"These runes will focus the energy in the crystals," Elijah said, shoving the journal he'd been scribbling in at him. "If we etch them into the clamps, it will encourage the particles to flow the correct way."

Thankful for the change in topic, I tuned out. Runes, crystals, and clamps were so far out of my realm of understanding it wasn't even funny.

Licking my finger, I flipped open the newspaper and scanned the coverage of yesterday's encounter with Morgana. The humans couldn't figure out what had caused the tremors but were having a good go at using science to bluff their way into calming the general public. So far, there'd been no aftershocks— something that baffled 'experts.'

"When you go through, there's no coming back," Dad said. "But how are you getting to the Druid homeland? Won't you need another portal?"

"I'm hoping someone will be there," Elijah replied. "I know a little of what to expect, but it's been a long time since they left this world. The way may not be watched anymore."

"I don't like the sound of this," Dad muttered.

"It's like Merlin to leave a failsafe incase the Naturals ever needed to contact him."

"You're taking one hell of a risk."

"With all due respect, Mr. Greenbriar, we're fresh out of options. If you have any other ideas, we're all ears."

For once, Dad had nothing to say.

"I'm not waiting," I declared, tossing the newspaper aside. "We go now or not at all."

"There she goes being a rebel again," Elijah quipped. "No respect for authority, that one."

I rolled my eyes. "Don't act so surprised."

"If we can create a stable connection, it may not be for long," Dad explained. "If it holds, even for a second, you'll have to go."

I glanced at Elijah. "We understand."

There was no room for hesitation. I didn't want to think about what would happen to us if we were caught inside an unstable portal when it closed.

The bathroom door opened and my mother emerged in a waft of steam.

"Nice of you to join us," I called. "Are you primped enough for the grand opening? Is there a ribbon to cut and a photo opportunity for the Natural newsletter?"

"*Madeleine*," she hissed.

I felt Elijah's hand on my leg under the table and settled. It was a cheap shot and my cheeks heated.

"We were working all night while your powers regenerated." Dad set down his coffee cup. "I think we're ready to attempt a portal. Come and see."

I glanced towards the workshop at the opposite end of the vault. A white sheet lay over something lumpy in the centre of the room, right where the scorch marks on the floor were located. I hoped I wasn't looking at a homemade pyrotechnics display— that wasn't a punchline I needed right now.

I left the newspaper behind and followed my parents.

Mum pulled the sheet off the lumpy pile and I stared in confusion at the tangled mess of car batteries, wires, and quartz crystals. I couldn't believe what I was looking at. It was so far beyond the realm of what I was expecting, I thought they were pranking me.

"What in the Light is all of this?"

"The portal," Dad said as he hauled up a wire archway that looked suspiciously like a trellis he'd nicked out of some poor human's garden. He began to thread wires through it as Mum clamped cables to the crystals.

"Are they serious?" I looked at Elijah, who shrugged.

"In the absence of a skilled Druid with all their powers, yes," he replied, standing beside me. "This is the next best thing."

"*Great.* All we need is a lawnmower travelling at eighty-eight miles per hour and we're on our way."

Elijah snorted and Dad shot me a forlorn look.

He'd obviously been working hard on this, no matter how ridiculous it looked.

"We'd almost solved Camelot's illusions," Mum said, "but we were missing one key ingredient…"

"We could begin to open a portal, but they were never stable," Dad added, surveying his handiwork. "Trying to harness all the chaotic energy of the mesh that binds worlds together was too much for us to handle."

"I don't think Naturals have the ability to control them," Mum said. "As much as we want to."

"What are you trying to say?" I asked with a shake of my head. "You can't do it?"

"That's the thing," Dad replied. "We can, but we need a Druid's…*Colours*…to stabilise the wormhole."

"This sounds more and more like a science fiction novel," I muttered, glaring at the car batteries.

Dad coughed. "Madeleine, do you think you can tap into your Druidic side?"

I glanced between my parents and my eyes widened. "Wait… Me?"

"I can't reach my Colours," Elijah said. "But don't worry, I'll show you what to do. It's rather simple."

"If it's so simple, wouldn't we be there already?" I asked.

"Creating a portal is one of the most difficult things a Druid can do," he told me. "Which is why Merlin was the only Druid I knew who had mastered them completely. Anchoring one once it's active is simple." Which was how he could travel through the portals in the archive.

"So, it's like focusing on one to see the destination?"

"No."

I wanted to fist my hands into my hair in frustration, but I swallowed hard instead. "I don't understand."

"I'll guide you," Elijah said. He reached into his pocket and handed me his nwyfre stele. "This should help."

I turned over the silver knife in my palm. The crystal set into the end sparked in the warm light of the workshop.

"Power comes easily to a Druid after a while, just like your Light as a Natural," he murmured. "Though shapes and angles help when weaving a prism, especially for the first time."

"Can I see those runes again?" Dad asked, holding out his hand towards Elijah. The Druid gave him his notebook. "Ah, so if I engrave these into the clamps… Bethany, darling." He wiggled his fingers at my mother, who began fossicking noisily in a toolbox on the bench.

It was getting a little mad scientist in here and I took a step back, clutching the nwyfre stele.

We were really going. That leap of faith I'd been mulling over was imminent and my stomach churned. Who knew what awaited us in the Darklands?

Elijah and I checked that we had all our weapons as my parents finished etching the runes and hooking up their strange power array to the arch.

"Ready?" Dad called out, holding onto a clamp. "Stand clear."

We all took a step back.

"Here we go!" He clipped the clamp onto a large battery and the lights flickered.

Power surged through the wires, filling the archway with static that made my hair crackle and begin to rise. To my astonishment, a portal began to flicker within the trellis.

"It's working!" Dad exclaimed as electricity popped and crackled. "This is the strongest one yet!"

"Madeleine, the anchor," Mum urged.

Elijah stood behind me, his body melding along mine. I felt his warmth and took a deep breath. He said it was simple, but we'd soon find out if I was capable.

"Call on your Colours," he said against my ear, his heartbeat thrumming against my back.

"How?"

"You've felt mine. Focus on that same feeling."

Yes, the cool, calming, blueness of ethereal nature. Shards of translucent Colour reflecting spirals and shapes. The unfurling of a newly sprouted seedling. The curl of a shell. The membrane of a wing. The refraction of Colour shimmering along a sunbeam. Water. Life. *Spirit*.

Warmth spread through my body and I held up the nwyfre stele.

"That's it," Elijah murmured, his breath fluttering along my neck. His palm moved down my arm, guiding the Druidic Colour into my fingers. "Don't be afraid of it. Let it gather…"

I softened as his touch circled my wrist and guided the stele through the air before the portal. Energy flickered within the archway, reacting to each sweep of the crystal.

Down, to the right, diagonally to the centre, diagonally to the right.

"I can't see anything," I whispered. "Am I supposed to?"

"Not until you seal the prism with your blood." *Oh yeah… the cutting part.* "Just a small cut." He pressed the end of the blade against my palm and a drop of blood bloomed crimson on my pale skin.

The rune flared, burning icy blue, and the portal flickered wildly before it stabilised.

I opened my mouth, but before I could formulate any words, the whole bridge shuddered. Elijah held onto me as the portal wavered.

Oppression radiated from above and I knew we were in deep shite. I could sense her essence and the same nausea I felt in the archive rolled through my stomach.

"*Morgana.*" I looked towards the ceiling as the tremor subsided. "She's above us."

Elijah frowned. "She must have sensed the portal opening."

"Then it's only a matter of time before she finds us."

"How can you…?" Mum shook her head and gestured to us. "Is the destination certain?"

Elijah smoothed his hand over the surface of the portal, sending ripples across the inky pool.

"What do you see?" my father asked. "The Darklands?"

"I see a black forest," he replied uneasily. "Its presence tugs at me…"

I sensed a similar urge to throw myself through the portal and shivered. "Do the Darklands call to Druids?"

"No. The homeland calls through them," Elijah replied, lost in his bewilderment. "I never thought…"

Mum nudged us towards the opening. "You have to go before Morgana blasts her way in here."

"You both have to come with us," I said, tugging on her arm. "Quick, before the ceiling collapses."

She pulled out of my grasp and I stared at her in shock.

"Madeleine, *go*. We can't leave this here for her to find. If she figures out where you've gone, she will follow."

I shook my head. "*She could follow anyway.*"

"We have to salvage something." Dad was gathering journals and bits of wiring, scooping them into a bag as the roof of the workshop began to crumble.

They wanted to stay so they could save their research.

"It's not worth it," I cried, tugging on her hand. "*Come with us.*"

"We'd just be a liability."

"I know we have our differences, but are your lives

worth this?" I jabbed a finger at the portal. "You can rebuild!"

"Listen…" Mum glanced at Dad, then turned to me, "it's not that we hate you, Madeleine, it's just… We don't understand what you've been through, but we're trying. All we want to do is protect you—even if it's from yourself."

"Seriously? You really want to talk about this *now*?" I asked, grasping her shoulders and shaking her.

A smile tugged at her mouth. "What better time than a life or death situation?"

I could see it in her eyes that they weren't coming and that no amount of pleading would change their minds. Numbers and equations were more important to them than their own lives. Research could be pieced together again, but try telling two strong-willed Naturals that.

Wind from the portal tore at our hair and I threw my arms around my mother's neck. "One day you'll understand."

Another impact rattled the foundations of South Bridge. Dirt and centuries' old mortar rained down on us.

"Madeleine, you have to go now," Dad said. "The portal is unstable. It won't hold much longer."

"Then once we're through, you have to run. *Promise me.*"

Mum nodded. "We promise."

I took a step back. "*You better.* I'm not finished giving you grief yet."

Dad slipped his arm around Mum's waist and smiled as the light from the portal shimmered across their features. "You wouldn't be our daughter if you didn't."

There was nothing else to say or do but for us to go our separate ways. Fate would take us where it must.

A third impact rocked the bridge, sending debris down from the ceiling. It was now or never, but I desperately looked back at my parents, hoping they'd reconsider.

"Go!" my mother screamed. "Go before it's too late!"

I cried out as the vault began to collapse in on itself, the ground shuddering violently.

Elijah took my hand and together, we leapt through the portal into the unknown.

12

———

I landed on pitch-black grass, wheezing as I drew in a breath of thick air. The portal flickered as it snapped shut, plunging us into darkness.

"Madeleine?" Elijah's hushed voice reached me through the haze.

"I'm here," I whispered.

The new world we found ourselves in felt oppressive, like the sky was weighing down on the land below. I hadn't had the nerve to look up just yet —I guess I was afraid of what I would find.

I choked back a sob as I recalled the last glimpse of my parents as the vault began collapse. I didn't know if they were alive, if they'd been buried inside the workshop, or if Morgana had killed them. We couldn't go back to find out—not until we'd found the Druids.

I regretted fighting with them. For not understanding. For being harsh. For being unforgiving. There were so many unsaid words between us and I didn't know if I'd ever get the chance to say them.

But if they were here, I knew what they'd want me to do—complete the mission.

I rose, my eyes opening.

We stood atop a dark hill, a cool breeze fluttered against our backs. Below, the Darklands stretched before us and above was a cloudless night sky. A forest clung to the valley, the canopy a thick carpet of indigo foliage.

Everything was black, and if it wasn't, it was slightly less black. The grass, rocks, trees, leaves, and sky were all the colour of pitch. The only thing that wasn't was the moon…or was it a sun? The way growing things seemed to reach for the silvery orb led me to believe it was the only source of light in this whole place.

I shook my head, not sure if I should be awed or afraid. This world was stuck in a constant loop of endless night and who knew what slunk in the shadows?

"This wasn't what I was expecting," I muttered.

"Me, on the other hand," Elijah quipped, "I was expecting far worse."

"I was expecting fire and brimstone."

"Not quite," he replied. "The stories are filled with tales of fierce beasts and twisted magic, but no flames."

I shot him a look. "Why are you only telling me this now?"

"I figured you knew. It *is* called the Darklands.

The name is kind of self-explanatory." He scanned the landscape in one long sweep. "Regardless, we need to move. The portal would have alerted everything for miles."

"You don't have to tell me twice." I nodded towards the forest. "First, a little cover."

We descended down into the forest, moving through the first layer of twisted trees. Trunks grew at sharp angles, zig-zagging into a thick copse that was hard to pass in some places. Branches entwined like braided rope, the inky black leaves sparkling softly with dew.

There was a strange primordial beauty about this place. The land that time forgot to drag out of the ooze and shine sunlight upon. Life had thrived despite the lack of warmth, finding a way to cling to the murky shadows.

But the more I stopped myself to listen, the more I realised I didn't hear any of the normal sounds native to a forest. There was no rustling in the undergrowth, no birdsong, no snapping twigs from passing animals. The Darklands had a stillness I found unnerving.

My fingers brushed against my arondight hilt and I was glad for its comforting weight against my hip.

Suddenly, Elijah grasped my arm and dragged me into the ferny underbrush. I opened my mouth to complain, but he pressed his finger to his lips, motioning for me to be silent.

I stilled, ducking down amongst the ferns, and cast my senses out into the night. I felt the presence of something alien and looked back the way we came.

A creature of shadow emerged over the rise, its essence floating in the air like ink in water. Its humanoid shape writhed around the hilltop, precisely where we'd been only moments ago.

Elijah stilled beside me, watching the shadow with sharp eyes. We didn't dare move while it writhed in the fading energy of the portal. A moment passed before a second creature joined it.

My fingertips began to tingle and I reached for my arondight blade. My palm steadied against the familiar feel of the hilt as I watched the shadow creatures pool together. Were they absorbing the echo from the portal?

We watched them in silence, ready to strike if they came our way. After a while, they seemed to have gotten their fill of residue and melted down the hillside, returning from where they'd emerged.

"What in the Light were those things?" I whispered, my spine crawling with the ultimate case of the heebie-jeebies. I didn't think they were demons necessarily, but they definitely had their own kind of Darkness about them.

"Whatever they are," Elijah replied, "the Druids would have rather risked facing them than the demons of the Dark."

"A comforting thought…*not*."

"Maybe they're shadow people," he mused.

I frowned. "Ghosts?"

"No, ghosts are human spirits. I'm talking about

shadows who live in other worlds, that you can only see out the corner of your eye. Menacing things, they are. They drain life and energy wherever they go. Maybe they originate from here?"

I shook my head as if to clear it. "It doesn't matter. We're not on an episode of *Ghost Adventures*. We need to find the way to the Druid homeland."

"I'm not going to ask how you know about that show."

I ignored him and rose, the pitch-black ferns rustling. "Where do we go now?"

"We follow our instincts," Elijah replied. "We both felt drawn here, so it stands to reason the Druid homeland will guide us to where we're supposed to go."

"I hope so."

I looked around the twisted forest and shivered. There was no telling what other creatures lurked out there, or if something intelligent waited for unsuspecting travellers to cross their path.

C'mon, Madeleine, I thought, *you've faced scarier things and lived to tell the tale. This is a walk in the park*. It was a little wishful thinking on my part. We were in another world where there was a whole new rule book.

Light didn't reach here, but perhaps, a few Colours did.

"C'mon," Elijah said, walking away, "this seems like the right direction."

Who was I to argue? He was one hundred percent Druid with an infallible compass.

I followed him deeper into the forest, shadows playing on my mind.

We forged a path through the Darklands, losing all sense of time and direction. Without the cycle of night and day, it was impossible to tell how long we'd been walking through this Light-forsaken forest.

Soon, we had to stop so Elijah could sleep.

I could bolster my stamina with my powers, but he wasn't so fortunate. I could give him some of my energy, but it wore off faster than either of us would have liked. Stopping was inevitable.

"I don't like this," Elijah said, looking around the woods. "There's nowhere safe to rest."

He was right. The landscape was twisted and full of dark corners, and we were made of Light and Colour—our presence alone made us beacons.

"I can go a while longer without sleep," I said. "I'll watch over you."

"I can keep going."

"We've been walking through this awful forest for at least two days. The air here is so heavy, even I feel tired," I told him. "You can't go much farther if you don't get some sleep."

Elijah frowned and sat amongst the bracken. I could tell he was thinking about what my father had said to him the day before we'd left. Without his Colours, he was as good as a human, and that made him a liability.

I nestled beside him, urging him to lay down. "Sleep. I'll be right here. The bracken is tall enough to hide us if another shadow slinks along."

"Just for a moment..." Reluctantly, the Druid curled up on the black earth and closed his eyes.

As Elijah drifted off, I began to see the truth in the Druid's stories about this place. The journey was perilous, but the homeland awaited. Merlin had guided the way, leading his people to the promise land. It was a rather religious tale when I put it that way but after a few days in this place, I was already a believer.

Still, we had no Merlin, so the ending to our story was uncertain at best.

Elijah had been asleep for no more than ten minutes when a snap echoed through the darkness.

He jerked awake as my head turned towards the sound. I listened, my senses brushing up against an ominous presence rustling through the undergrowth.

Something was out there. Something *big*.

I reached for my arondight blade, my palm brushing the cold iron hilt. Elijah knelt, making as little sound as possible and passed his finger to his lips. He could sense it even without access to his powers.

Knowing we couldn't linger, we moved away, slinking through the forest. Twisted branches and distorted trees hindered our path, making progress slow. I looked over my shoulder but was unsure if I was seeing the creature who hunted us or if it was just my rising fear playing tricks on me.

Grimacing, I took the rear guard. I was used to doing the hunting, not being hunted.

We forged on, our footsteps as silent as our breath, but the unknown creature followed us no matter what path we took. It had our scent and we didn't know how to shake it. Normal rules didn't seem to apply in this reality, and we were forced to press on.

Soon, the forest thinned, and we emerged into a rugged expanse of what looked like fractured moorland. Rock jutted up from the tundra, splintering towards the black sky like a honeycomb maze. Above, the moon radiated an eerie silver glow, illuminating the mist which had settled amongst the wild terrain and stretched the shadows to impossible lengths. I wouldn't risk it on a bad day. Down there, it was a horror movie waiting to happen.

Elijah looked at me and grimaced. "We have no choice."

"We can lose it amongst the rocks," I said in an attempt to sound unfazed.

Branches snapped in the forest behind us and we scurried into the mist before whatever pursued us caught us in the open.

The deeper we fled into the unknown, the more fractured the moors became. Soon, we were lost in a maze of jagged rock and boggy grass.

I brushed my hand across the face of the stone and realised it was hardened like glass. No, not glass…crystal. Enormous points of smooth, planed faces emerged from the solid crust of the planet. Most points were broken and scarred by unknown forces, but some were intact, the perfectly symmetrical formations shimmering in the muted light.

"These aren't rocks, they're smoky quartz," I murmured.

"And obsidian," Elijah added. "Fused together."

Crystal could hold energies beyond our reckoning, but in this place…? It could either be a good thing for us, or a terrible way to die. If an electrical storm came through here, we'd be cooked alive. That's if the shadow people didn't find us before the creature stalking us did. They could use this place as a battery, just like they'd sucked up the residue from our portal.

I pressed my palm against the obsidian. "There's no fire in the ground."

"There must have been once. Obsidian is volcanic glass and it's everywhere. This world wasn't so dark once upon a time."

"Crystallised lava," I mused. This place must have been a mass of super volcanos that spewed forth oceans of lava hundreds of billions of years ago. Life, no matter how twisted, took a long time to develop, especially under those conditions.

A deep, guttural roar echoed through the maze, the sound bouncing off the crystalline walls.

I grasped Elijah's arm and together, we moved on. There was no time to ponder the meaning of it all when we might not even make it out of here alive. There were too many people counting on us on finding Avalon to linger.

It wasn't long before we lost all sense of direction.

We moved through the maze, taking whatever path was presented to us. The only way was forwards.

I didn't know how long we'd been moving through the crystals when they opened up to reveal clear sky and a sharp drop. I skidded to a halt and pulled Elijah back as pebbles rained over the ledge, clattering down, down, down…

"Shite," I hissed, looking into the void below. It was a dead end.

Sensing danger at our backs, I turned.

A pair of glowing silver eyes shone out of the darkness, the creature's low growling rebounded ominously off the enormous crystals.

Trapped.

Elijah and I were perfectly still as it lumbered towards us, emerging from the shadows like a waking nightmare.

Finally, we came face to face with our pursuer.

The unknown hunter had to be at least eight feet tall, its body made of pure muscle. Shaggy black hair hung limply from its hide and atop its wolf-like head was another three feet of pointed antlers. I barely registered the razor-sharp claws on its hands and feet as my startled gaze took in the strips of rotting flesh hanging from its horns like grotesque Christmas decorations.

It seemed like we'd had the pleasure of meeting the apex predator of the Darklands.

The monster's lips curled back with a snarl, showing us its pointed grey teeth and indigo gums. It was going to eat us, then. *Great.*

We stared at one another for a long moment, the creature's silver eyes holding a primordial intelligence that chilled me to the bone. This thing was a killing machine and knew nothing else.

Time slowed as I sensed its muscles coil and I pushed Elijah out of the strike zone.

The monster lunged, and a claw grazed my side, tearing at my flesh. I cried out and rolled, hurtling through the monster's legs, drawing its ire away from Elijah. I tumbled and pushed to my feet, my heels digging deep into the soft ground.

I leapt forwards, my boots popping free with a squelch. My arondight blade flashed, and I grasped one of the monster's antlers. It bellowed and reared its head, wrenching me into the air.

I almost lost my grip on the velvety surface, but I used the distraction to swing. I pushed myself forwards with a pulse of Light and landed on its back and almost gagged at the stench. Whatever this thing was, it reeked of death and decay.

I fisted my hand into its furry hide and brought my sword down. Sparks flew as the blade struck.

Black, congealed blood spurted from the gash as I rose my arm to strike again. The monster roared in agony and bucked violently, trying to throw me off.

"Madeleine!" Elijah shouted. "The cliff!"

I threw a hasty glance to the side and cursed. Blue sparks ignited as Elijah attempted to hobble the beast, but it wasn't going to be enough.

I flipped, grasping the monster's antlers. I wrenched down, using all the power I could pool into my arms. The beast's jaws snapped, its breath rancid and hot as it tried to crunch down on me, but it didn't stand a chance.

I was protected by its antlers, caged at the edge of the cliff. We had a chance to slay it, but we had to strike fast or not at all.

Elijah leapt onto its back and the monster jerked and began to thrash.

"I can't hold it!" I cried, my grip slipping. "It's too strong!"

My boots inched towards the chasm and I caught sight of a blue flash in the corner of my eye. Elijah was clear. Now I had to deal with this monster once and for all. There was only one way I could see us escaping, and it was right behind me.

The beast pushed against me, inching us towards the bottomless drop. I could sense the vast nothingness at my back, and quickly went through my options. *Think, Madeleine, think!*

I only had seconds to spare.

I let go of the antlers and dropped off the cliff. The monster hurtled over the top of me and I grasped rock, the sharp fragments cutting into my palms. With a cry, I pushed myself up and over, rolling away from the edge.

The creature shrieked, its claws scraping as it desperately tried to climb back onto the ledge. Its black, congealed blood oozed over its hands and over the rock, making it too slick to grab hold.

Reaching for my power, I flung a burst of energy

towards the flailing beast, giving it one final push into the abyss.

It let out a screech that tore at my ears and tumbled downwards, crashing against jagged outcrops before disappearing into nothingness. All sounds of its fall were swallowed whole, leaving Elijah and I in absolute silence. It was like nothing had happened—except for the rancid blood coating everything.

We stood at the cliffs edge and peered into the darkness below.

"Do you think it's dead?" Elijah asked, wiping his sticky hands against his trouser legs.

"I don't think anything could survive that fall," I panted.

He sighed and held up his hands. "What I wouldn't do for a shower right about now."

He was right. We reeked like rotting flesh, but I hadn't seen a single water source since we'd arrived. We'd have to stink for a while longer.

"We better get out of here while we still have the chance." I glanced over my shoulder at the jagged crystal fields. "I feel like we're close to something familiar."

Elijah tugged at my jacket, pulling it away from my side. "You're bleeding."

"It's nothing that won't heal." I shook him off. "I want to be far away from here when its friends come looking. One was bad enough."

We made a hasty retreat, disappearing amongst the crystal monoliths before our luck ran out.

13

———

Elijah and I moved through the crystal maze, emerging on the outskirts some hours later.

Rock and smaller smoky quartz points littered the ground, making the way just as treacherous as what we left behind.

If it wasn't for the crystals, I wasn't sure we would have seen the monster at all. We certainly would have if it'd caught us in the forest. Its ability to camouflage itself was terrifyingly impressive.

My boot slipped on a shard of smooth crystal and I stumbled, sending a sharp throb through my side. Righting myself, I pressed my hand against the claw mark and bit my bottom lip. The tear in my flesh wasn't healing.

When Elijah realised I'd stopped, he paused and came back. "Are you all right?"

"I'm tired, is all." I waved him off. "And the ground is slippery."

He glanced at my side. The Druid wasn't buying it.

"My abilities seem to work differently here," I said, preempting any unwanted sympathy. I was supposed to be the strong one—the Triune who fought celestial beings and survived. "I'm not as powerful. It must be the dense atmosphere."

"Or the creatures are stronger than those on Earth."

I shrugged. "That too." The faint pull that had been guiding us tugged at me once more. "C'mon. The way should be easier now."

Elijah nodded, casting one more glance at my side.

We'd gone another mile before I realised my fatigue wasn't from lack of sleep. I wiped the back of my arm across my sweaty forehead, wondering why I was so cold when my brow burned.

Naturals didn't get sick. The worst I'd had was a throbbing headache and mild nausea. I assumed this is what it *really* felt like to be an immune-compromised human…and it was awful.

What was on that monster's claws? Poison?

"Sit," Elijah said, guiding me to a flat rock. "Catch your breath for a moment."

My knees crumpled underneath me and I slumped down, the stone cool to the touch.

I took a deep breath. "I feel like we're close. We should keep going."

Elijah squatted beside me. "It won't hurt to rest a while."

"It will," I snapped. He recoiled slightly, his brow creasing. "I'm sorry, I… This place…"

"I know," he murmured. He slid his palms over my thighs, his touch comforting in the pitch landscape. "The shadows are oppressive here. Without sleep, they seem to grow."

Breaking out into a cold sweat, I scraped my hair off the back of my neck and combed it forwards over my shoulder.

Elijah felt my forehead. "You've got a fever."

"We just need to find the Druids," I murmured. "And some clean water and some medicine…or *something*." Elijah didn't reply. I frowned when I saw he was focused on something over my shoulder. "What?"

"Someone's watching us," he whispered.

The hairs on the back of my neck began to stir and I cursed softly. I should have sensed them, but whatever was poisoning me was draining my abilities.

I stood, wavering slightly. There was no way I was going to sit down and wait for another monster to attack us. I was Madeleine Greenbriar, and I wasn't going to die without a fight.

I drew my arondight blade, but before the sword could engage, Elijah shouted a warning.

"*Madeleine!*"

Light erupted around us and Elijah leapt towards me. His arms encircled my body as threads of electricity wound around us, weaving splintered geometric patterns over our clothing and skin.

I gasped as frozen shards struck deep, numbing

my entire body. The power flared around us, revealing an intricate spiderweb trapping us in place.

Movement shifted the air and figures began to emerge from the fractured Darklands. Ethereal blue light shimmered over humanoid shapes as they formed a circle around us.

They were clad in black robes, blending seamlessly with the landscape. It wasn't until one of them lifted their hood and revealed their face that I realised it was a woman.

Elijah's eyes darted to mine, the only part of him able to move, and I knew we were thinking the same thing. *Druids*. It had to be.

I couldn't sense anything, let alone feel beyond the poison inching through my veins. Whatever was festering on that monster's claws had cancelled out my abilities—all three of them.

"Who are you?" the woman demanded. "*State your purpose.*"

I tried to open my mouth, but it was as if my lips had been superglued together. Elijah, on the other hand, seemed to be able to speak just fine.

"We're seeking your help," he said. "The help of the Druids."

"You ask for help with an insult?" Her cool gaze fell onto me. It wasn't hard to see she had a problem with my presence. I *was* an expert in being a target for hostility.

"You know what I am," Elijah said. "I wouldn't break any covenant unless—"

"Then why do you travel with this creature,

Druid?" she sneered in distaste. "Why would you stoop to share the journey home with…*this*."

"What…?" Elijah began, his brow creasing.

"She means me," I drawled, my lips loosening. At least I'd been granted the right to sarcastically fight for my honour.

"That's not a creature," he stated with a huff. "That's Madeleine Greenbriar, one of the greatest Natural warriors I've ever known." The Druids stared blankly at him. "She's defeated greater demons." Our audience continued to wait. "She threw a giant beast with rotting antlers off a cliff a few hours ago."

"I don't think they're impressed by how well I can kill things," I murmured. "I think you should give up while we're slightly behind."

The Druids began to stir at the mention of the predator we'd faced on the crystal cliffside.

"You fought a relic?" The woman appeared aghast at the prospect. So that's what the monster was called.

"It was either that or be its lunch." I snorted. "We've come here at the command of the Regula," I went on, "the rulers of the Naturals. We've come from Camelot."

The Druidess narrowed her eyes. "Camelot?"

"*Yes*. We reclaimed it from the Dark, but it's in danger. Our whole world…" A wave of unfamiliar weakness slammed into my mind.

I let out a garbled cry and all the strength faded from my body. The only thing that held me up was the Druid's binding prism.

"What are you doing to her?" Elijah demanded. "Let us go!"

"This isn't our doing," the woman said, raising her arm. "Unlock the prism." Oddly, she didn't seem concerned about my condition. It was as if she'd seen it before.

Elijah caught my listless form as the geometric shapes faded and lowered me gently to the black heath.

The Druidess knelt beside us and lifted my T-shirt. She studied my wound for a moment, then rose with a sigh. "She's been marked."

The Druids began to back away, melding with the shadows.

"You're leaving?" Elijah demanded, his voice echoing off the crystal and rock. "Why?"

"The Darklands have claimed her," she replied cryptically.

"I'm bound to her," he snarled, cradling me in his arms. "You can't leave her in this place without abandoning me."

The Druidess shook her head. "It isn't that simple."

"I've longed for this moment for eight centuries…" he murmured, tears misting his eyes, "but I will walk away if it means saving her life."

"Eight centuries?" The woman's expression faded into shock. "You're…"

Elijah looked up at her. "I am Caradhan… And I've come to claim what's mine."

"If what you say is truth, we would allow you to pass, but it's too late."

"What do you mean?" he demanded.

"The Darklands have chosen her," she replied. "If she wants to travel into the homeland with you, she must pass their trial."

"Who's trial?" I rasped.

"The Old Ones." The Druidess looked down upon me. She had no sympathy whatsoever. "You must face them."

"I'm *poisoned*. This isn't some—" I coughed as my vision blurred around the edges. "This isn't some crazy ritual."

"The Darklands guard our world and in return, they claim the unworthy. Fall behind and become marked. Prove yourself to them and they will let you pass."

"She didn't fall behind," Elijah hissed. "*She fought back.*"

"It doesn't matter." The Druidess backed away, merging with the line of robed Druids. "The trial must run its course. We cannot stop it."

I moaned, clutching Elijah's shirt. "I can do it. I can—"

"Madeleine," he crooned, stroking my hair, "fight it and come back to me. *Fight it.*"

"I…intend…to…" My eyes drooped and the Darklands faded.

———

I stood in the back forest.

A clearing opened up around me, the sky obscured by an indigo canopy. A trillion eyes stared down at me, waiting. I could sense them pierce my flesh and plunge into my soul. *Curious.*

I wondered what these mysterious Old Ones made of me.

Movement stirred at the edge of the wood and Bethany Greenbriar slunk out of the shadows, her eyes glowing with white-hot anger.

I blinked, confusion muddling my mind. "Mum?"

Her arondight blade engaged, silver sparks rained across the clearing like tiny fire sprites. Striding towards me, she rose her sword. *She meant to attack.*

I backed away as she advanced. "What are you doing?"

"Fight back, Madeleine," she demanded. "No daughter of mine dies without even trying."

I snatched my arondight blade from my belt and the shaft snapped into place, igniting with holographic fire.

We clashed, our blades sparking as they collided. We locked together and she pushed back against me, her lip curling with distaste.

"Even your Light is poisoned," she hissed. "It's muddy…just like your soul."

"Mum, *stop.*"

Her boot collided with my knee and I crumpled to the ground with a cry. She struck me with the flat of her blade and I was on my back, my temple throbbing.

"You should never have been born," she growled. Blackness dripped from her eyes, oozing down her cheeks in congealed blobs.

"H-How can you say that?" I exclaimed.

"You were a mistake, Madeleine. A mistake I aim to rectify." She raised her blade, meaning to strike me through the heart.

This wasn't real.

I rolled to the side, the blade barely missing its mark. My mother screeched in anger and I kicked her legs out from underneath her. Flipping, I was on my feet in a flash while she lay flat on her back.

I struck, jamming my knee into her chest and my sword at her throat.

"Don't. *Move*," I snarled. "You are not my mother."

"*Monster.*"

"I know we have our differences, but we'll never work them out if we fear what each other is going to do. Look past the *what* and see the *who*. I'm still Madeleine and you're still my mother. Our connection is deeper than any Darkness."

She hissed and her face began to morph into an inky black snake. Fangs darted towards me and I sliced downwards, taking the creature's head clean off.

I rose, my hands covered in gunk, and wiped them against my trousers. "Ugh."

"Are you okay?"

At the sound of Elijah's voice, I cried out, "Are you really here? Did I pass?"

He embraced me, his lips finding mine in a blistering kiss.

"I'm so glad to see you," I said, breaking away from his passion. "You'll never guess what those stupid Old Ones made me do."

Elijah wasn't listening. His touch became forceful, his hands moving underneath my shirt. He forced his way inside my trousers, and I began to panic.

"Elijah, *stop*…"

He pushed me against the tree, my back scraping the rough bark. Grinding his body along mine, he wrapped his hand through my hair and pulled my head painfully to the side.

"Don't you want me, Madeleine?" he demanded. "Don't you want me to take your virtue? It's painful at first, but then it feels oh so *good*…"

"*Stop*. This isn't you."

"You will be the death of the Druids," he murmured, his breath hot against my neck. "You cannot leave the Darklands."

"This isn't real," I said, my heart thrumming a wild beat. "You'd never do this to me, Elijah. *You'd never hurt me*."

"But you'd hurt me without a second thought," he said, his voice grating. "You can't even tell me how you feel. You can't even say the words, Madeleine."

I choked back a sob, but I couldn't stop the tears from falling. He was right. I was afraid.

"You think you're protecting yourself, but you're only hurting everyone around you." His fingers curled around my neck. "If you love someone, *set them free*…"

I gasped as his grip tightened. I'd always kept Elijah at arm's length, giving him just enough to keep him hooked. I'd saved his life and vouched for him, he'd declared himself to me in the deepest way he could as a Druid, and I couldn't even say three little words—three little words that were the truth, but forever stuck inside.

This wasn't real.

My vision blurred as the life began to slip from me. What use was it? I couldn't die—not from this—but I'd be deemed unworthy.

I'd be doomed to wander the Darklands alone for eternity. Would I become a shadow or would my Triune soul damn me to become something far worse?

"I love you, Elijah. I do, but this isn't real." My hand closed around the hilt of my cold iron dagger.

His grip loosened slightly. "Don't lie to yourself, Madeleine. You cannot convince yourself to believe false realities. *Not here.*"

"My fear lies with your reply," I told him. "How can I hear it when you're not Elijah?"

The Druid's malicious grin faded.

I snorted. "See? You're not so clever, are you?"

I plunged the tip of the dagger into his back, the blade sinking through flesh as if it was soft butter.

Elijah's eyes widened in shock and he gasped. A thin drip of black blood speed from between his lips and he stumbled back a step.

My fingers slipped away from the dagger and I

watched as he swatted at the hilt that protruded from his back.

"You…" he coughed, black blood gushing from his mouth, "you killed me."

"I killed my fear," I said, trying to separate him from the real Elijah. "I'd never hurt the true Elijah and if I did, I'd make it right."

He fell to his knees with a strangled sob. "Understand, creature. *You—*"

Fake Elijah never got to finish what he was saying. Gale force winds wrapped around me, stirring out of nowhere and blotting out the forest. My hair blew in all directions while debris battered my exposed skin.

"I'm going to fight Morgana and I'm going to win!" I shouted into the void. "I'll even fight you if I have to! *I'm not afraid!*"

The unworthy became shadows.

I shivered, recalling the creatures that writhed around the hilltop sucking up tenants of our portal. There was no way I would become one of those things. *Never.*

"*I'm not afraid!*" I shrieked. "*Do your worst!*"

The ground tore away from under my feet and I fell through the darkness.

My eyes flew open and I sat up with a strangled cry.

"Madeleine!" Elijah's hands cupped my face, drawing my consciousness back to the present.

"The Old Ones have released her," the Druidess declared. "Open the portal."

I grasped Elijah's face as the wind began to rise. My fingers studied every rise and fall and felt every shred of warmth in his skin.

"You're real," I rasped. "You're here."

"Yes, I'm real." His brow creased. "What in the world did you see?"

"The portal is open," the Druidess declared. "We must pass through before the shadows come."

"Can you walk?" Elijah asked me.

"There were trillions of them," I said, dreamily. "They all looked into my soul."

"That's a no, then." He grimaced and gathered me into his arms. Rising, he carried me through the portal without looking back.

It was time for him to go home.

14

I was lying in a lumpy bed when I opened my eyes.

I stared at the whitewashed ceiling and breathed in the earthy scent of woodsmoke with a tang of herbs. It felt homely and comforting.

I sat up and scanned the room, finding a simple set up of a fireplace, bed, and side table. A woven rug covered the floorboards and simple art hung over the mantle, where a quartz crystal glinted in the warm light.

It reminded me of a simple seventeenth century English cottage.

The door opened, letting a waft of crisp air inside, and Elijah walked in. I gave him the once over, wondering where he'd gotten the flowing white linen shirt and tan-coloured breeches. If he had a kilt, he'd look exactly like a rugged Scottish Highlander in a romance novel. He still wore his combat boots and belt with his dagger and arondight hilt.

"What *are* you wearing?" I asked, looking him over.

"Proper Druid garb," he replied with a smirk. "Ethically made from all natural fibres."

"Well, it's better than black tactical gear after the Darklands." I laughed, glad to be back in the light.

"How are you feeling?"

"Better. Everything feels like normal." I lifted my shirt and smoothed my palm over my side. "I'm all healed."

"It scared the life out of me when you collapsed," he admitted. "What did you see?"

"I had to slay my fears," I told him. "But the specifics are a little…*muddy*.

He fell silent, not knowing how to reply. I wasn't about to tell him the scraps I remembered, either. Somehow, the Old One's trial seemed sacred—a personal pilgrimage to the core of my being.

After a moment, he said, "When you came back, you were as high as a kite."

"Was I?"

He laughed and shook his head. Maybe I shouldn't be asking for details.

"You've come to claim what's yours?" I asked, changing the subject. "A little dramatic, don't you think?"

"It's not a declaration of war," he replied with a smirk. "I was telling them I intended to claim my rightful place amongst the Druids."

My heart twisted. "Which is…?"

"Madeleine, it was just a way to get us in. They

were going to leave you in the Darklands to fend for yourself."

"Until I collapsed."

"Yeah," Elijah sighed, "until that…"

"Your true name?"

He grimaced.

"I get it," I told him. "Names have power. I've felt it."

"I should have told you."

I shook my head. "No. True names should never be uttered to anyone. Ikakantor used one of mine in front of everyone. I had no choice. You still have power over yours."

"It doesn't matter," he murmured. "True names only hold sway when not in our own lands."

I stilled. It made total sense now. That's why Naturals didn't have the same problem, even though our powers were closely related to both the Druids and the Dark. But maybe Naturals didn't have them at all, what with being a band of humans bestowed with gifts by a Celestial. It was something I'd have to ask the Lady of the Lake…if I ever got to meet her.

"Merlin will want to see you."

"Merlin?" I asked, my gaze darting to Elijah's. "He's alive? How do you feel about that?"

"Indifferent."

"C'mon," I argued. "After he turned his back on you? He condemned you to centuries of demonic control!"

"What good would it do?" He shrugged. "It seems you hold all the anger for me."

"I can't believe—"

"Madeleine, we need him on our side. Don't forget what we left behind on Earth."

Morgana, Camelot, the Naturals, and the threat of extinction. He was right. I should focus my anger on the task at hand.

"Caradhan is a nice name," I murmured, running my fingers through his hair. "It's strong."

Pounding on the door broke us apart.

"Madeleine Greenbriar!" a female voice boomed. "You've been summoned."

I made a face. "Polite, aren't they?"

Elijah snorted and picked up a pile of clothes off the side table. "You better get dressed. This is the chance we've been waiting for."

"Do you think he'll help us?" I asked as I climbed out of bed. I held up the green tunic the Druids had given me and grimaced. It wasn't form fitting *at all*.

Elijah hid an amused smile. "There's only one way to find out."

I pushed through the door and stepped out into a different world.

A woman stood before me, dressed in the dark-coloured clothing of an elfish warrior. A mossy green tunic was tucked beneath simple leather armour that scaled over her slender shoulders, and brown linen trousers clung tightly to toned legs. Simple leather boots rose to her knees, the laces pulled tight.

It was the Druidess from the Darklands who'd been so *friendly*.

Now we were in proper sunlight, I could make out her waifish features in greater detail. Her heavy black hood concealed sparkling chestnut hair which cascaded over her shoulders like soft waves rippling over the surface of an ancient lake. Shocking emerald eyes stared at me from underneath impossibly long lashes and I felt a sting of jealousy in my heart. She was beautiful, but not just any kind of beautiful. She was transcendent.

"Oh, it's you," I drawled.

The woman looked me over, though her emerald eyes didn't reveal her thoughts.

"I am Eliorla Draheann," she said. "I lead the *neach-gleidhidh* in the Darklands."

The language was familiar somehow, though it sounded like she was clearing her throat. "Is that Scottish—"

"Gaelic," she interrupted. "Parts of your Earth came with us to the homeland. The *neach-gleidhidh* are guardians, keepers."

"I see." The languages must have mingled when the Druids reconnected—Irish, Scots, and British.

"I'm also Caradhan's sister."

I froze as if her words had slapped me on the face. Elijah's *sister*? "How…?"

"I was born here," she stated. "I never set foot in your world. I grew up with tales of the brother I lost to your war with the Dark."

"Does Elijah know? What about your parents?"

My heart was breaking and hopeful all at once. If his family was here, then he deserved to know them. But what if he wanted to stay?

Eliorla snorted, her lip curling. "You ask a lot of inappropriate questions for a *mèirleach*."

I didn't know what a *mèirleach* was, but it didn't sound good.

"Merlin is waiting," she said, her cool tone signalling that she had nothing more to say on the topic—to me anyway. "Follow me…and do not stray."

I bit my tongue to stifle a sarcastic comeback and hurried after her long strides.

The Druid homeland was a world of unhindered nature—green and brilliant, dusted with Colour and ancient energy unspoiled by the industrial pollution of humanity. The people simply lived amongst it as their ancestors had on Earth. Melding with the land, they'd thrived in peace, growing and regaining the power they'd lost during the war with the Dark.

The settlement reminded me of a mixture between a Medieval village and an Iron Age Celtic encampment—though for every simplified building, there was a complex magical enhancement that put much of modern humanity to shame. No one needed WiFi, electricity, or smartphones here.

Runes and geometric patterns were etched everywhere. Most seemed to have a purpose— lighting, cooking, heat for an iron working forge, irrigation, and healing—though others were for decoration while some promoted prayer.

The people wore clothing made from linen and

leather, and jewellery fashioned out of everything from crystal and bone to gold and silver. Now that I'd noticed it, I caught glimpses of clear quartz points buried in the lintels of many of the houses we passed.

Curious glances followed our progress through the settlement and I even caught scraps of conversation—none of it sounded good—but most Druids seemed preoccupied with other things.

A group of women were seated around a wooden table, weaving colourful flowers into a long chain—baskets laden with even more blooms lay at their feet. Children ran back and forth, carrying parcels and gifts. The men were lugging firewood and hunters were preparing freshly slain deer and curing their hides and antlers.

We'd reached the edge of the settlement before I realised it and I bumped into Eliorla, who'd stopped in front of me. She glared in annoyance.

"Sorry. It's just…" I nodded towards the commotion. "What's everyone preparing for? A party?"

"Merlin awaits." The Druidess jabbed a finger at the path. It wound up the hillside and disappeared into a copse of trees, but I focused on her hands, curious. A thin spread of pale white lines marked her skin.

She caught me staring and lowered her arm, her scowl deepening. "Mer—"

"*Merlin awaits*," I complained, stepping past her. "Don't worry, I'm going."

I hurried along the path, eager to get this long-awaited meeting under way. I moved through the trees, shivering as an unknown force tugged at my sleeves. It wasn't malevolent—it felt as if something old was curious about my arrival.

When I emerged at the top of the rise, I found a stone circle, though it was a rather small one. Six flat rocks had risen in perfect alignment, their jagged edges pointing towards the sky.

Within the boundary was an elderly man. His wiry white hair was impossibly long, hanging halfway down his back, but he stood with the strength of youth in his bones.

Merlin.

Impossibly boundless power leeched off his skin, harmonising with the world as if he was one of the elements. I lingered at the edge of the stone circle, unsure if I should enter.

The man turned, his blue eyes shimmered like sapphires. He looked every bit the wise old wizard from the Arthurian legends—impossibly long beard, bushy eyebrows, wise wrinkles, flowing robes…the whole bit.

"So, you are Madeleine Greenbriar," Merlin declared, "the Triune."

"It looks like you're organising a party," I retorted. "Somehow I doubt it's for me."

"Caradhan is the first Druid to find his way to the homeland in centuries," he said, looking over the settlement. "It's cause for great celebration."

"You do know who he is, right?" I turned, half wanting to strike the Druid down where he stood.

The other half knew it would be foolish to take on Merlin with the thought that I could win.

He studied me with cool eyes. "Yes."

"You turned your back on him," I hissed. "You abandoned him to the Dark, and now you welcome him home without the slightest apology? *I can't believe you.*"

"You speak of things you do not understand, child."

"I know longing," I said. "I also know what it's like to have family look on their own children as worthless monsters. Asking for help is hard but being abandoned by those we love is worse."

"I could not help him. If he came to me today, I still could not."

"I hope that's not an excuse."

Merlin narrowed his eyes. "Caradhan was bound within his mind. It is a sacred space the Druids cannot reach even if we wanted to." He gave me a knowing look, but it wasn't exactly brimming with added approval. *He knew.*

I wondered if Elijah had already been to see the illustrious leader of the Druids. How else could Merlin know I'd gone into his mind to free him from Ikakantor?

"The Darkness poisoning him is gone, but he can't reach his Colours," I said. "Can you help him get them back? You owe him that at least."

"It is not a matter of repaying a debt."

"Then what is it?"

"You've been through many trials on your path

here," he said, ignoring my question. "Why have you come? It's a dangerous journey through the Darklands for a Druid's Colours. That cannot be all."

I may as well cut to the chase. "Morgana," I replied. "She's risen."

For a split-second, I was sure I saw Merlin ignite with blue flame…but I blinked and it was gone.

"*Explain yourself*," he demanded.

Fearing his wrath, I told him everything—the end of the war and Mordred's last stand, Human Convergence, Camelot, the Dark's last gasp, Scarlett and Wilder's condition, what we'd found in the archive, Elijah's struggles, and finally, Morgana's escape. There was no hiding a single shred of our history if we wanted the Druid's help. Besides, he was Merlin. Once upon a time, he'd stood beside Arthur Pendragon at the height of Camelot's power as an ally and friend. We revered him, just as we revered the Lady of the Lake.

When I finished, Merlin remained silent. He was so still, I wondered if he'd died of boredom. It *had* taken a long time to bring him up to speed…or maybe he'd fallen asleep with his eyes open.

I waited. Sounds from the settlement drifted up the rise, carried by the fragrant breeze—jasmine, cherry blossom, and the tang of citrus.

Finally, I decided to give the Druid a little verbal prod. "You had to have known a celestial being was imprisoned under Camelot."

"Arthur and I had one chance to imprison her,"

the Druid said. "One chance to hold her forever… and now you say she has escaped?"

I nodded. "I fought her myself and barely survived. That's why we need to speak to the Lady of the Lake. Morgana is determined to have her revenge on the Naturals and once she has it, she will burn our world to the ground."

"Our world?"

"It was your home once," I told him. "I don't know why the Druids came to Earth to begin with, but you were our friends and we will always regard you as such. We've come to ask for help."

"Avalon is sealed," he said, his tone sharp.

"You of all people know how to reopen it."

"If it is as you say, the way must remain closed." Merlin's expression darkened and I caught a glimpse of the true power hiding behind the face of the old man…and it was terrifying. "It's a curious thing, don't you think? For a being made of all three races of your world to come here and demand to see *her*. To believe you know the secrets of the Druids. To accuse us of abandoning Caradhan. Then to ask us to reveal our greatest secrets to save a world that betrayed us."

"Betrayed you?" My heart skipped a beat. "We never—"

"The Lady of the Lake entrusted Arondight and Excalibur to Arthur and Lancelot, and their fickle human hearts almost drove us to extinction. We helped the Lady of the Lake restore the Twin Flames and lost much because of it. Our responsibility for your world ceased when Scarlett Ravenwood left Avalon as Arondight."

He wasn't going to help us. I could see the anger in him rise in shards of unearthly flame.

"What do you want me to say, Merlin?" I asked. "What would you have me sacrifice?"

"The power *you* have, Madeleine Greenbriar, was stolen from us."

I swallowed hard, all my insecurities and guilt rising to the surface. He was right. The Druids had become collateral damage in a war of the Naturals own making. They owed us nothing, and here I was asking for more. What I'd become—because of Scarlett's *honest* mistake—was the ultimate insult. A Druid had died horribly at the hands of the Dark in order for me to exist.

Now I understood what *mèirleach* meant—*thief*.

"I never intended for this to happen," I blurted, my stomach rolling. "I never wanted to steal anyone's powers. I was a mistake."

"Perhaps, but perhaps not."

Shame heated my cheeks. "I'm trying to do the right thing. I just…"

I was failing miserably. What in the Light was I thinking? I'd waltzed in here all arrogant, assuming Merlin would just smile and open the portal to Avalon. I hadn't thought it through. The Druids had suffered so much because of us and here we were, dragging them back into another war, this time with a *celestial being*.

"I see Philomena in you," he said after a moment.

"You have her gifts. The primordial prisms call to you."

I blinked and pressed my palm over my heart. "Philomena? Is that…" *Shite, could things get any worse?*

Philomena was Gilhana's sister. *The* Gilhana who'd hidden herself in time so she could safeguard Arondight. Philomena died protecting her…or so she'd thought.

"Gilhana's sister," I whispered.

Merlin nodded. "Gilhana passed, living peacefully into old age, believing her sister died saving her from the Dark. Perhaps it was for the best she didn't know what became of her."

Philomena, the Druidess who'd become the Grey Lady thanks to the Dark's twisted experiments. She'd died for Arondight, not the abomination I'd become. Everything I was, was a slap in the face to everyone who'd ever died to protect our worlds—the Druids, the Naturals, and even the Dark.

Morgana was right. I shouldn't exist. I shouldn't even be here demanding things from Merlin.

"And what would that achieve?" the Druid asked. "You alone were able to stand before Morgana. Fate has brought you here for a reason that is yet to reveal itself."

I scowled. "How do you know that's what I was thinking?"

"Perception," he replied simply.

I rolled my eyes. "Perception?"

"I'm told you passed the Old One's test."

I nodded. "Yes, but what does that have to do with anything?"

Merlin didn't reply, waiting for me to understand his meaning on my own. Apparently, leaving threads hanging was a Druid thing. Scarlett had written about their tricks when she'd chronicled her adventures for the Codex. Taking the journey on one's own was far more important than the destination. Being handed an explanation was cheating.

"The relic marked me," I said. "It tried to kill me, but I got to it first."

"Relics are ancient beasts," Merlin stated. "They have twin hearts that must be pierced at exactly the same time in order to still them."

I hesitated. "So, we didn't kill it after all."

"I'm afraid not."

"Even after it fell into a bottomless chasm?"

"The reality of the Darklands is twisted. Time and space don't flow as they do here, or back in your world, nor do the creatures live within the bounds of nature's restrictions."

I paused. "It meant to mark me, not kill." It'd gone straight for me because it knew what Elijah was.

"I suspect so," Merlin mused. "Curious, don't you think?"

"You're a curious creature yourself, Merlin," I stated with a huff. "I don't know if you're going to kick my arse or braid my hair."

"Do not fret, child," the Druid told me. "My grievances with the Naturals are old. We have enjoyed centuries of peace in our homeland, though leaving was one of the more difficult things I've had to do. Arthur was one of my most trusted friends and I was powerless to free him from the rift."

"You did that for your people," I murmured. "If you hadn't, the Druids would be no more and Elijah… Well, he would be on his own."

Merlin proceeded to give me the silent treatment for what felt like the millionth time. I had no idea if he was on our side, against us, or simply neutral on the whole thing. Earth wasn't his concern anymore, but he had to have some feelings about the world he'd been such an integral part in building. That was the thing I was banking on.

Still, my hopes were dying with every passing moment.

I drew in a deep breath. "If you won't help us with Morgana, will you help Elijah?"

Merlin studied me, impassive as ever. "Caradhan's Colours are buried deep."

"Is that a yes?" I grimaced with uncertainty.

He gestured to the view before us. "Be still, child."

There was something I wasn't understanding, but by now, I knew better than to keep pressing the wrong buttons.

"Merlin?"

He raised a bushy grey eyebrow in amusement. He'd anticipated my rush of questions like he'd seen it before. He must have suffered the same bombardment when Scarlett met him—she liked to ask a lot of questions, too.

"Who are the Old Ones?"

"The custodians of a reality far older than any us can comprehend."

"Oh, is that all?" I chuckled and looked over the settlement.

Merlin's lesson was lost on me and I feared for the world I'd left behind. Contemplating the meaning of the universe and everything in it made my brain hurt. It was a little more than I'd ever be able to comprehend. All I knew was life and death—and death was what awaited my friends back on Earth if Elijah and I failed.

"Merlin?"

"Be still, Madeleine," the Druid murmured. "Things are rarely as they seem."

15

That evening, the sun set and the Druids rose.

A million and one scents drifted through the air—flowers, perfumes, cooking food—fragrant and heady. Music ebbed around bonfires, while singing and laughter dotted through the melodies like staccato notes.

It took me the rest of the day to realise Merlin had been teaching me how to connect with my Druidic side. Now that I understood, I was having trouble unravelling how I was meant to do it...and what I would find when I did.

Despite my cluelessness, Merlin had accepted me and by his decree, the Druids were bound. They welcomed me the fireside, but I could sense the veiled trepidation in their curious stares. Eliorla had called me a *mèirleach*, a thief, but I'd never taken Philomena's Colours on purpose.

It seemed I would be forced to defend myself forever. I was a Triune, but I belonged nowhere.

I wandered through the unfamiliar celebrations, my Druidic third drawn to the shimmering Colours. I wondered where Elijah had disappeared to—he *was* the man of the hour. I hadn't seen him since that morning, and I had so much to tell him about my odd meeting with Merlin.

I mean, how old was he anyway? The Druid was just as grey when Scarlett met him in the twelfth century and that was over eight hundred years ago. I looked around the settlement and noted there weren't many Druids who were a day over middle-aged.

I stood just outside the glow of a fire pit, watching as a group of young women dressed in flowing white dresses—complete with flower wreaths wound in their silken hair—laughed and danced around the open flame. Their bare feet skipped lithely over the soft grass, leaving sparks of holographic Colour in their wake. I gaped, transfixed by the simple beauty.

Two men sat just outside their circle, one beating a deerskin drum, the other playing a stringed instrument that looked like a lute. It was a scene straight out of a fantasy novel.

One of the women caught me staring and broke away from the dance, her shimmering blonde hair cascading down her back. Everyone was so intimidatingly beautiful here, and I felt pale and sunken in comparison.

"Dance with us," she said.

My cheeks heated and I shook my head. "Oh, no I couldn't... I-I mean, I can't dance. I'm terrible at it."

"A strike with a blade is the same as dancing without," the woman said, tugging on my hands.

Afraid they might be offended by my refusal, I allowed her to drag me into their circle. The women laughed and joined hands, guiding me in a ring around the fire. I stepped awkwardly, skipping over the sparks of Colour.

"Take off your boots and feel the earth," another woman suggested, sensing my uneasiness.

They grasped my arms and eager hands took my boots off for me, tossing them aside.

"See?" the first woman asked as my toes curled into the soft heath. "Much better!"

They erupted into giggles as the men began to beat on their drums once more. They set a fast rhythm and I was drawn into the dance.

The flames flared as I twirled, my heart hammering in my chest. A breathless exhilaration overcame me and my lips curved upwards.

I caught sight of a familiar face as I circled the fire. *Elijah*. Wait until he saw me!

I made to call out to him, but the words died in my throat as I saw Eliorla walk beside him. They were talking fiercely, their heads close together so they wouldn't be overheard.

Breaking away from the circle, I melted into the surrounding party, intent on following them. They stopped beside a cottage away from the celebrations and I darted around a corner, keeping out of sight.

I lingered in the shadows, only feeling slightly guilty for eavesdropping.

"She has the very thing that ruined your life inside her," Eliorla said. "Caradhan, she is Darkness."

"She is also Light and Colour," Elijah snarled.

"She is a *mèirleach*."

"*Do not use that word*. Madeleine did not steal anything. She was a victim, just like I was. Eliorla, she risked everything—imprisonment, torture, exile, *death*—to save my life. She has asked for nothing in return. *Nothing*. Would a creature of the Dark do that?"

The Druidess scoffed and crossed her arms over her chest.

Elijah tugged on her sleeve. "You know I love her."

She turned and glared. "But does she love you, brother?"

"She loves me in her own way."

"It's not enough and you know it. She would keep you from your people and take you back to her world to face certain death at the hands of the Celestial."

I bit my bottom lip as annoyance flared. How did she know about Morgana? How much had Elijah told her without me knowing? They *were* family, but they didn't know one another…

"Death is not certain," he hissed. "Wouldn't you fight to protect those you care about? Of course, you would. You walk the Darklands with the *neach-gleidhidh* for fun."

Eliorla scoffed, "I don't enjoy it. I—"

"*See*." There was a rustling sound and he added, "You carve runes into your skin."

"I need them to survive the Darklands."

"You don't need them, Eliorla. You *want* them."

"What I do to my body is my business. The *mèirleach* will live forever and leave you behind," she argued. "She cannot give you children or love. You say she feels the same, but I have not seen it. Without your Colours, you're doomed to a mortal life."

"Merlin will help me," he hissed.

"He will ask a price," Eliorla said. "And you know what it will be." *To stay in the homeland.*

I leaned my back against the wall and breathed deeply. Was Eliorla right? Were my feelings for Elijah selfish?

Elijah deserved to be with his people—*his family.* There was nothing but war and pain waiting for him on Earth. There was no guarantee we would win against a being as absolute as Morgana. Here, he had a future.

"There you are."

I turned at the sound of Elijah's voice and plastered a smile on my face. "Some party, huh?"

"I guess." He rose an eyebrow when he saw my bare feet. "Where are your shoes?"

"Uh…" I glanced over my shoulder and shrugged. "Their location is currently unknown."

"How did things go with Merlin?"

"Well, I uh… I don't know exactly." I swallowed the lump in my throat. "He said *a lot*, but Druids never say anything plainly."

"Why give a yes or no when you can deliver wordy philosophy instead, huh?"

"At least you know how to say yes or no." I

glanced over his shoulder, and thankfully, Eliorla was nowhere in sight. "Your sister's a ball of sunshine."

"Maybe my attitude wasn't all Dark after all." Elijah laughed and sheepishly ran his hand through his hair. "A Draheann family trait."

There was that twist of guilt in my heart again. Man, it hurt. "Speaking of family. Elijah, I—"

"My parents are gone," he said, interrupting before I could go on. "Eliorla said they passed a decade ago."

"A decade? Well, they lived a long time…" *Lame and insensitive to boot.*

"Apparently, I have some cousins who survived the trek through the Darklands," he added, graciously ignoring my awkward comment. "They have children of their own now, but they live in other villages. Eliorla is my only sibling."

"Wow," I murmured. "So, you have a whole brood of blood relations you didn't know about?"

His smile faded as though he sensed the tension I was holding in my heart. "I don't know them. Without my Colours, I don't really…" he cleared his throat, "I don't really fit here, either."

"Don't say that," I said, laying my hand on his chest. "Merlin will help you. I know he will."

Maybe the price was worth it. He would be safe, but not only that… Elijah would be complete again. He'd have everything that was stolen from him returned.

Elijah lowered his gaze. "Time will tell, I suppose."

I scoffed. "If anyone deserves to be multi-coloured, it's you."

He cupped my face and I sunk backwards. A flicker of confused hurt flashed through his emerald eyes and I grabbed his hands.

"Do you want to find something to eat?" I asked, concealing my conflicted heart. "I'm sure you're starving. It's been a *long* couple of days. Besides, I might find my boots."

"Sure," he said as I led him through the gathering. "Sounds great."

<hr>

The following day, Elijah was summoned for secret Druid business, so I was left to my own devices.

I must say, they trusted me a lot more than the Naturals had. I could wander where I liked and talk to anyone who was brave enough to reply. Apparently, my dancing last night had been the icebreaker that split a crack in the word *mèirleach*.

I wasn't sure how long we were going to be here, but only one thing was certain—I had to get Elijah's Colours back, no matter the cost.

An elderly Druidess was attempting to teach me how to weave when Merlin appeared. It was an odd situation to find myself in—a warrior who could face fearsome beasts at the helm of a frightening loom. I'd tangled just about every thread there was to tangle, much to the Druidess' frustration.

"If you were attempting to make an intricate ball

of knots, then you've succeeded," was Merlin's greeting. "Well done!"

"I'm much better with swords," I grumbled.

"Walk with me, Madeleine. It's such a lovely evening." Outside, he pointed towards the sky, where the sun had burned orange and purple across the horizon. "The first stars appear."

"The constellations look like Earth's," I mused.

"Curious," the old Druid said with a smile. "Don't you think?"

"I'd rather say it was obvious. We are on an alternate Earth, aren't we?"

"Or you came from an alternate *Thríbhís Mhór*."

"What is that? Your name for the homeland?"

"The triskele of earth, sea, and sky," he said with a nod.

"Oh, a triskele!" I exclaimed, finally understanding something. "The Celtic symbol of three conjoined spirals. Of course! You guys love your symmetry."

Merlin twirled his beard, the motion almost comical. "Celtic, is it?"

We strolled through the village, passing Druids going about their work. Merlin greeted them all by name, taking the time to stop and ask after their loved ones or some task they'd been struggling with.

The leader of the Druids had a lot of time for his people. It was an admirable quality.

When we reached the woodlands at the edge of the settlement, I began to wonder where we were going exactly. I hadn't seen Elijah all day and I was eager to know how he was.

"There will be a great ritual this night," Merlin declared, as if he could read my mind. "We will call upon Caradhan's Colours."

"Wait," I said with a gasp. "You're helping him?"

"There was never any doubt we wouldn't." *What was I saying last night about difficult Druids?*

I dreaded asking the next question, but Eliorla had planted a seed of doubt. "What is your price then? What did you ask him for?"

"Price?" Merlin stopped. "It is not for me to exact a cost for calling a Druid's Colours. Not for Caradhan."

I swallowed hard. "So, you won't make him stay?"

"That choice is up to him. I suggest you ask him about it."

"Why didn't you just say? I've been stewing over it for a day. *Will he? Won't he?*" I sighed dramatically. "What about Morgana? Can I press that button yet?"

Merlin smiled and guided me along the path. "There will be time to consider your request after the ritual."

"Is that where we're going?"

"You ask so many questions, yet you don't hear the answers."

Why were Druid's so cryptic? They never said anything plainly—everything had a moral and a journey, and never a yes or no. At least Elijah was direct.

I followed Merlin along the path and up another

rise, knowing we were headed for the ritual site. I pursed my lips from asking the question, hoping I was learning something from the old sage.

As we reached the top of the hill, my mouth dropped open in awe at the sight before me. I wasn't sure what I was expecting, but the reality was far more impressive.

The stone circle was an enormous structure, spanning at least a hundred metres from the thick, grass-covered outer ditch and mound, to the upright stones in the centre.

It reminded me of Stonehenge—even at three times the size—though this monument was well cared for with all its stones intact, even the horizontal lintels. Time and changing populations had ravaged its twin on Earth, but here it was, still well traversed by the Druid's daily use.

Unlike Merlin's stone circle above the settlement, which was raw stone risen in its natural state, these blocks were chiselled and shaped in perfect rectangles. The bluestone was threaded with veins of glittering crystal and obsidian, reminding me of the dangerous and ethereal landscape of the Darklands.

A large outer circle surrounded a smaller monument of blocks arranged in a horseshoe formation, and other stones dotted the ground between the outer ring and the ditch, marking important alignments with the stars and the rising and setting of the sun.

As Merlin guided me towards the circle, I felt a familiarity that echoed into my soul.

"Welcome to the Brionglóid henge," the Druid said.

I gazed at the stone circle, unable to look away. "It reminds me of something familiar."

"Many of these stones were gathered from the Darklands," he explained. "They celebrate our link with the Old Ones and with our deepest selves. The connection between us, the world we inhabit, and the multitude of realities beyond. It is a place of dreaming."

"Am I welcome here?" I asked. "I mean, I hear what the other Druids say about me…that I'm a thief."

Merlin smiled. "In time, once they have completed their journeys, they will understand. No matter how you came by Philomena's Colours, you are part Druid now. Your soul sings, Madeleine. If this was her fate after so much suffering, then it is a good one. Her memory lives within you."

Her memory lives within me. It seemed like something I should remember.

"Am I to take part in the ritual?"

"No. We must weave a delicate prism and it is not for the faint of heart…or the clumsy of fingers." He gestured for me to sit on the hillside. "You must remain perfectly still," he warned. "Do not utter a word or Caradhan's Colours may be lost to him forever."

"All right," I said as I sat on a spongy patch of grass. "Clumsy fingers will sit here." I wiggled my digits at him.

Merlin smiled, taking on the demeanour of a loving grandfather. I kind of liked him in a strange roundabout way—even when he was being vague and infuriating.

"Thank you," I said.

"You're most welcome, Miss Greenbriar." He paused a moment, then declared, "You have a most bramble-esque treelike name." *What a strange thing to say.*

"Do I?" I mused. "I never noticed."

16

Silver light spilled over the henge as the moon rose over the Thríbhís Mhór—the Druid homeland.

I sat on the hillside, frozen on place, watching for movement below. My gaze flickered over the stone circle, marvelling at its size. Why had the Druids left this place to begin with? It seemed like paradise after the turmoil I'd grown up amongst on Earth.

The air stirred, halting my introspection and I tensed. The Druids were coming.

Elijah was led into the stone circle by a group of six men. Their steps were slow and purposeful, as if they walked a choreographed path. I could feel the hum in the air as the Brionglóid henge sensed the rise of Colour in the air.

While they wore simple white shirts and slacks, Elijah was bare-chested. A rune had been painted across his scars in a shocking blue, though I couldn't tell the shape of the symbol from this distance. I wondered if it was an anchor for the ritual—a place for his Colours to focus their return.

He knelt upon the altar stone in the centre of the henge, his head bowed, and remained perfectly still. The other men formed a semi-circle behind him, all facing the way they'd came.

Then points of warm light pricked into life from out of the shadows, as Druidesses in ivory-coloured dresses made their way along the path. Two dozen in all, their hair was free and flowing, and each wore a crown of woven white flowers.

I could see the handles of their torches were twisted and carved branches, and the flames were surrounded by what appeared to be rippled glass. Though as they moved, the glass glinted with an arcane light. *Prisms*.

The world hushed around me as if everyone on the planet held their breath. Nothing stirred—the forest was silent, the wind fell, and the earth ground to a halt. Not even a single echo came from the village.

The Druidesses held their torches aloft and bowed, raising their left arms in a graceful wave, the sleeves of their dresses fluttering with the subtle motion. As they brought their heads up, they began to move with elegant steps.

Their dance wove an intricate path, their bare feet leaving behind strands of shimmering Colour which built up as they twisted and turned around the henge. The Druidesses fluttered like arcane spirits, calling upon a higher power. Who it was, I didn't know, but I hoped they knew the way to the Colours hidden inside Elijah's soul.

I barely took a breath as the hairs on the back of my neck stood up. I was witnessing something sacred, and even though Merlin had welcomed me here, it felt forbidden given who I was.

My heart was full to bursting for Elijah. This was who he was.

I didn't know how long I watched the Druids weave their prism, but when the sun began to rise, I felt a pull in my soul so powerful, I wasn't sure I could fathom the importance of what I was witnessing.

Rich, burnt orange light fell upon the henge, bringing the stone to life. Crystal and obsidian sparkled like precious jewels as the Colours of the ritual reached their crescendo.

The Druidesses came together in a tight circle around the altar and held their torches to the sky. The prism flared and floated over the inner henge before settling like a gentle net over Elijah's exposed skin.

The ritual was complete, and the women spirited away from the stone circle, followed closely by the men.

Elijah remained as he had since he'd knelt on the altar stone, unmoving as if he was deep in prayer. Finally, as the prism faded, he rose and turned his face towards the rising sun.

His Colours had been called…and now it was time to wait.

I exhaled, lost in the hope, romance, and whimsy of the Druid's magic.

I sat on the hillside for a long time, leaving Elijah to his meditations. It didn't seem right to go down to the henge lest I interrupt something important.

Instead, I tangled myself in my thoughts as I watched the sun rise. I quickly realised I knew nothing about the Druids, and the things I did weren't remotely close to the truth. How would I describe them to the Naturals if we ever made it back to Earth? I wasn't sure there were enough words to convey the things I'd seen. Well, enough of the *right* words, that was.

When he was ready, Elijah left the henge and disappeared into the woods. A few moments later, he appeared on the path before me.

I smiled as he approached. He seemed calm, as if a power had risen in him. He'd pulled on a rough-spun green tunic that covered the rune on his chest. The edges of the sacred symbol peeked out from underneath the collar, bright blue against the pallor of his skin.

He sat beside me on the rock and said, "Merlin said I'd find you here."

"Do you feel any different?" I asked.

"Anyone would after that," he replied. "I don't know if my Colours will come back. I just have to wait and see."

We watched the sun climb a little higher before he spoke again.

"You've been quiet lately."

I shrugged. "It's a lot to take in."

"Madeleine, you know you can tell me anything."

I smiled. "You're too perceptive sometimes."

"What's bothering you?"

"Lots of things. The Darklands were bad enough. That vision was creepy and it's not even taking fighting that relic into consideration. Then there's everything with my parents. Let's not forget everything else that's happened."

Elijah frowned. "I don't think that's it. Do you?"

"What else could it be? All that stuff is pretty heavy, you know."

"Yes, but since we've arrived here…"

He had me there. I guess this place was bringing out the Druid in him for better or worse.

"I thought Merlin would ask you to stay in return for calling your Colours," I admitted. "I didn't want you to lose your chance to get them back."

"So the other night, you thought you'd pull away from me?"

"Things are complicated," I murmured. "With Morgana, my powers, the Naturals, Camelot… I don't even know if my parents got out of their workshop alive. We could return to a ruined world. It could be too late."

"That's the chance we took when we stepped through that portal. We both knew the risks."

"I know, but now we're here… I didn't realise…"

Elijah stilled, his emerald eyes giving away nothing. "Realise what?"

That you shouldn't be forced to choose between your people

—your family—for a mèirleach *and a world that might hate you for your past forever*, I thought.

"If what you want is to stay, then I will support you," I told him. "You've been through so much, Elijah. I only want the best for you."

"What about you?"

I bristled and shook my head. "This isn't about me."

"Of course, it is."

"Please don't," I whispered. "It was such a beautiful night…"

Elijah looked away, focusing his gaze on the henge. Maybe we were too different. He was so in tune with who he was and what he wanted, it made me feel little more than a child. Technically I was, even though I'd come of age the day I'd graduated from the Academy.

"Merlin is going to take you to Avalon," he said, breaking the silence between us.

I straightened. "He is? Since when?"

"I don't know. Why he does the things he does isn't always clear."

Avalon. My mind tumbled over and over, so many thoughts and troubles fighting for my attention. I was going to meet the Lady of the Lake, the celestial being revered by my people, and all I could think about was Elijah's happiness.

"Something is coming to an end," he murmured. "I can feel it."

I didn't have it in me to reply. Anything I could have said wouldn't have made things better.

"We better go back to the village," Elijah said. "Merlin will come when he's ready."

"And not a moment before."

A flicker of a smile pulled at his lips. "Precisely."

I rose and Elijah stood beside me. Maybe it was just me, but he seemed taller.

"This is what we've been hoping for, Madeleine." He cupped my face, his fingers brushing over my skin ever so slightly. "Morgana won't just stop at our world." *Our world.* "She'll come for this one, too."

"Revenge is a bitter pill," I whispered.

"And a war which no one wins."

"Those are wise rods," Merlin declared.

My heart leapt into my throat and I turned to find the Druid standing behind us.

"You frightened the life out of me," I complained, pressing my palm over my heart.

"Hardly," the Druid stated. "You're alive right now, so there's plenty of life remaining. Are you ready?"

I blinked.

Elijah nudged me. "It's time, Madeleine."

"Now?" I exclaimed. "I thought you'd make us jump through a few more hoops first."

Merlin grinned and delivered his seed of Druidic philosophy. "When one can bend time and space, time can still be of the essence." He seemed rather pleased with himself for someone so wise.

"That feels like a paradox," I declared.

"Paradoxes are no laughing matter, but they are a debate for another time perhaps." Merlin raised his bushy grey eyebrows and held out his hand, gesturing for me to follow. "Come."

I stepped forwards, but Elijah didn't move. "You're not coming with us?"

"With the ritual complete, Caradhan must work on guiding his Colours," Merlin said with a shake of his head.

I glanced at Elijah. "You don't mind?"

"No," he replied. "After seeing Morgana up close, I'm not keen to meet another Celestial, even if she is the Lady of the Lake. Besides, Merlin is right. The ritual was only one part of calling my Colours. I have more to do before they can return."

I hesitated. I knew there was nothing I could do to help him, but I wanted to give him the world anyway. Elijah had risked everything to make it this far—just as I had—and leaving him behind didn't seem right.

"The Lady always has a reason for every action she takes," Merlin told me. "She recognises the sacrifices Caradhan has made to come here, but it is you she seeks."

"Yeah, cause that's not ominous at all," I muttered.

The old Druid gave me a knowing look. "It is trust she offers in order to meet you in the flesh." *And I knew all about trust.*

My gaze met Elijah's and he smiled. "You can tell me all about it when you get back."

"Okay," I murmured. Turning to Merlin I nodded. I was ready.

Merlin led me down the hill and we walked

amongst the standing stones of Brionglóid henge. The monolith was even more impressive up close with its enormous upright blocks of sparkling stone. Each had to weigh at least thirty tonnes, and there were over a hundred and fifty making up the bulk of the circle.

I'd watched the Druids weave a complex prism on this very spot only hours before. The ground felt charged underneath my feet and I wondered if that's why Merlin had been waiting for this moment. Did he need a little juice to open the way?

I looked up in awe, struck by the otherworldly essence that flowed through every part of the ritual site. It was as if every element merged into one here, buzzing and simmering like a giant battery of arcane power.

"This is the portal?" I asked as we stood in the centre of the structure.

"There is no portal. The way is sealed," the old Druid replied. "This is a scared site, full of Colour and starlight. It's as good a place as any."

"So how are we getting there?" I looked around the stone circle, but we were alone.

Merlin chuckled and waved his palm in the air. "The portal is not fixed in place like the ones you have seen before, Madeleine. I am the only one who knows the prism to guide us into Avalon." He swept his hands through the air, weaving and twisting, then let out a satisfied *humph*. "Ah, there it is."

I raised my eyebrows, wondering if he was slightly senile, when the air shimmered before the altar stone. A portal snapped open, the surface rippling grey. The henge reflected back at us like oil on water and I blinked in surprise.

"You make it look so easy," I said.

"I've had many lifetimes to perfect my prisms," he said matter-of-factly. "Weaving time is familiar to me as it is to breathe the air of Thríbhís Mhór." He held up his gnarled hand and gestured for me to step forth. "Come, Madeleine. The Lady awaits you."

I glanced uneasily at the portal. "You're not coming?"

Merlin inclined his head. "You have nothing to fear, my child. This meeting has an air of destiny, don't you think?"

"I don't know anything about destiny," I murmured. "All I know is that answers are waiting. Answers I need to help save my world."

Merlin smiled, the emotion conveying something a little more than I could comprehend. Maybe one day I would understand the ways of the Druids, but for now, Avalon awaited.

"Wish me luck," I said.

"You carry the Light of your people and the Colour of mine, Madeleine Greenbriar. You do not need luck."

I gave him one last look and nodded. Luck was nothing without action.

Turning towards the portal, I stepped through the veil into Avalon.

17

The air carried the scent of lilac and primrose.

I opened my eyes and blinked as bright sunlight filled my vision. I held up my arm and drew in a shaky breath. Avalon was known as Ynys Wydryn to the Druids—the Isle of Glass—and now that I was looking at it, I knew why.

A lush, emerald green forest stretched into the valley below, shimmering with refracted light. It glittered like crystal and the lake beyond was smooth like glass.

Avalon was a perfect piece of ancient Britain, locked away in space and time, untouched by the technological advances of humanity. It was the sanctuary the Lady of the Lake made for herself and the Druids after the cataclysm that let the Dark into Earth.

The last Naturals to come here were Scarlett and Galahad…and now me.

I turned, noticing I was standing on a path that

wound up a small knoll. It reminded me of an ancient Anglo-Saxon burial cairn—a mound covered in a thick layer of springy green grass—but it wasn't a place for the dead. Far from it, actually.

A lone figure awaited me on top of the rise. A Celestial made of pure Light.

I walked along the path with my hands buried in the long sleeves of the rough spun tunic the Druids had given me. After growing up with a thousand and one interpretations of her likeness, I wasn't prepared for the real thing. I didn't know how I would react when our gazes met.

As I reached the top and came face to face with the Celestial who'd created my people, my breath was taken away.

The Lady of the Lake was pure starlight. Her hair reminded me of spun silver, each strand shimmering when she moved, and her skin was so fair it was almost transparent. Where Morgana was pure fire and agony, the Lady was grace and spirit.

I couldn't move as she walked towards me. Her white dress flowed around her, fluttering like soft feathers of Light. I didn't believe in angels, but that's exactly what she looked like.

Suddenly, I felt like a grubby urchin dressed in rags.

"Madeleine Greenbriar," the Lady of the Lake said, her gaze passing through my body and piercing my soul. Her voice was a whisper brimming with essence—a bottomless lake of energy.

"I had no idea…" I whispered, wishing I'd combed my hair at least. "You're…"

"We have been called many things," she told me. "Celestials, Celestines, angels, Annunaki, gods, and goddesses. We are the universe, born of starlight." She gestured to the valley below. "Welcome to Avalon."

I stared at the iridescent vista, lost for words. All the questions I'd thought to ask her had tumbled out of my mind, and the trials Elijah and I had face in the Darklands seemed like a fairytale. I was disconnected.

"I know why you've come," the Lady said with an understanding smile. "Merlin has been to see me, but you and I have time. Avalon is a place where the passage of things ceases for a short while if I will it to be so."

"Then let's cut to the chase, shall we?" I stated. "Arondight and Excalibur are trapped in an endless coma—they won't wake while Morgana is free. But that's not our only problem. She is hellbent on revenge for the torment she suffered. My world will come to an end before she is satisfied, and I won't let her destroy everything we've vowed to protect."

The Lady of the Lake held out her hand towards me. "Show me."

I hesitated at first, something about coming into contact with a celestial being had me on edge, but I pushed away my fears and slipped my palm against hers.

Her touch was cool, yet I felt the warmth of her power as it leeched into my body. She saw what I had seen, knew what I had known, and suffered what I had suffered. Now she knew, and there was nothing left for me to explain. The answers were now hers to give, if she chose to help me.

She was not like Morgana, that I was certain of.

The Lady lowered her gaze as she let me go, and I began to wonder if she had something to do with the Celestial ending up in the vault under Camelot. She looked awfully guilty about something.

"Merlin and the Naturals imprisoned Morgana, but did you… Did you help them?" I asked.

"Morgana's strength makes it impossible for me to exist in the same reality," she replied. She was avoiding the true answer.

"But you helped them?" I prodded.

"I gave them the means, but I was unable to be there."

"Scarlett said they couldn't exist in the same reality as Morgana. It's the same for you, isn't it? That's why you left the Naturals behind on Earth?"

"Yes. They needed to survive on their own and amongst them, I was weakened. If calamity came, I would not be able to help. I knew there would come a time when I must leave forever, and I could not leave them without protection."

"That's why you gave the Naturals Excalibur and Arondight?"

She nodded. "I was able to remain for a time while their power was within the swords, but once the cataclysm came, I was torn away completely."

"And now Morgana has broken free."

"And I am powerless to help you…save for one last offering if you will have it." The Lady rose and lifted her hand. "I told Scarlett we are not creatures of creation or destruction, but it seems I was wrong. Morgana has proven that. This time, it must be the end."

She walked across the grass, her footsteps lithe on the lush grass. My breath caught as tiny plants began to sprout where her feet tread, unfurling into tiny white blossoms. Their centres shone bright yellow, smiling up at the sun.

Kneeling, the Lady picked one of the blooms and rose, cradling it in her palm as if it were a newborn child.

"This is the key," she murmured, her fingertips tracing over the petals.

"A flower?" I asked raising my eyebrows. It was pretty and all, but one blossom was barely larger than my thumbnail. "That's what's going to kill Morgana?"

"When the first of my kind came to reality, they grew where they walked." She offered no other explanation, but it was in no position to argue. I'd seen the blossoms rise for myself.

Cradling the bloom in her hand, I watched in fascination as tiny pinpricks of Light rose from her skin. She nudged the flower into the air and it hovered, defying the laws of gravity. The Light twisted around it, then flared.

When the spark faded, I was surprised to see a shard of clear crystal encasing the flower, a silver chain dangling from its tip. It was beautiful, but deadly.

I watched it spin, my mind turning a little more chaotically. "If there was a way to end Morgana, why did you let Merlin and Arthur imprison her?"

"I believed she could be redeemed," the Lady replied. "She wasn't always evil. I had hoped Morgana could find her place in the universe and flourish, though it seems I was wrong to put my faith in her." Locked away in darkness, her hatred had only grown.

"Power corrupts," I whispered. "And absolute power corrupts absolutely." How ironic it was that a human had uttered those words. They were universal to all species and it was why they were forced to imprison Morgana in the first place. I didn't need to know the details to understand. The Naturals seemed to walk hand-in-hand with extinction-level events.

"Take it," the Lady murmured, waving the crystal towards me. "It is the one thing that can end her immortal life and return her essence to the stars."

I grasped the crystal by the chain and I watched it spin, transfixed. All things had an end. Even starlight could be snuffed out.

I sighed. A flower was one thing but using it to destroy Morgana was another. How did we even get close? How did we use it? Approaching an enraged Celestial was suicide, even for me. Ramona had warned me about my abilities not being absolute. If Morgana wanted to kill me, she could.

"I don't see how I'm supposed to use this," I said.

"Morgana's powers are unfathomable. No one can get close to her."

"It is possible, but you must know her."

Frustration tugged at my Dark side and I shook my head. "Know what?"

"To understand Morgana, you must understand me," she explained. "Though I fear even I am subject to the deterioration Morgana has suffered."

I frowned. "Deterioration?"

"The Celestials weren't always as you've known us to be. Once we were a formless entity, our presence holding the fabric of the universe together. My mother and father became tired of watching life unfold and not experiencing what they nurtured, so they took on flesh and bone. I was made of their union, though I was not the only one of our kind to be 'born'."

"Was Morgana born, too?"

"No. Morgana was among those who chose to take on physical form, my parents weren't the only ones."

"So you're humanoid?"

"Something like that," she remarked. "I am restricted by my creation, which is why I linger in Avalon."

"Are…" I took a deep breath. "Well, aren't you lonely?"

"My parents were not prepared for the ferocity of human emotion," she replied. "Nor what would become of their children."

"So the isolation stops you from becoming overloaded?"

The Lady nodded. "I am not a true Celestial. I've never known true freedom from flesh and bone." She smiled, the power behind her simple emotion made me giddy. "I presume you know something of this."

I pressed the heel of my palm against my chest. "I was an accident."

"Natural, Druid, and Dark. A child of everyone, belonging to none. When she took human form, Morgana was alone and didn't understand how to cope with her new reality. Her path took her in a dangerous direction." *And she deteriorated into madness.*

I swallowed hard, piecing together what the Lady was trying to tell me. "Power and emption corrupted her."

"She turned to Darkness."

Darkness. "I don't understand… We always thought the One created the Dark. He was their source of power. Since the rift closed and Scarlett and Wilder destroyed him, they've been dying out."

"No." The Lady of the Lake shook her head. "Only the strongest remain because Morgana still exists."

"Morgana?" I whispered. "But that would mean that she…"

"I made the Light and Morgana made the Dark."

I rose and turned towards the valley, numb to the truth. It was worse than we'd ever known.

"You helped us destroy the Dark," I said. "You gave us the Twin Flames. If Morgana was the source of it all, then why let it get to this? You knew she was under Camelot and it was torn apart! Why didn't you say something?" I threw my hands into the air. "And don't spin me some shite story about redemption, because even I know she is incapable of it. She is twisted beyond recognition. *You could have ended it all.*" The Lady of the Lake stood before me, silent. "You could have told Merlin, given him the flower, then he could have returned to Camelot."

"And descend into the jaws of the Dark?" the Lady asked. "You would have had him sacrifice the last of his people to save your own? He created a pact with the Darklands and he alone ensures the continued existence of the Druids." *I guess I knew why Merlin was still alive then.*

"Then someone else… Someone else could have…"

Her cool hand cupped my cheek and her gaze captured mine. "Madeleine, we cannot change the past. We can only heal the present so the future can come to pass."

"The Naturals?"

She inclined her head, her hair shimmering. "The only way I could heal the present in order to protect the future."

My head swam with revelations and I could hardly piece them together. The threads were so tangled, I was having trouble straightening it all out. Where did I fit into all this? Was it yet another path I wasn't allowed to walk on because of my Triune soul? Or was I here because of it?

"There's still so much I don't understand," I began, my voice shaking. "If Morgana created the Dark, how can I stand before her? How can I stand before you?"

"You are Triune. You walk in both worlds, but you also embrace a third. It is that part of you which allows you to come to Avalon…while also standing before Morgana."

"The Druids. They're the bridge between worlds."

The Celestial nodded. "They are the weavers of time and space. They embrace nature and reality like no other creature the Celestials have ever encountered."

"Your kind didn't create them?"

"They are an ancient race, one entwined with the very beginning." The Celestials didn't create the universe, they were a part of it, and just like everyone else, they answered to a higher power.

The Old Ones. Merlin made a pact with them to cross the Darklands, a pact that was still upheld to this very day. The stones at Brionglóid henge. The trial I faced to pass through the portal. The shadows of the unworthy…that was the price of protection. The Druids were the children of the Old Ones, though nothing came for free.

I couldn't believe I hadn't seen it until now.

There were forces in play that I would never understand. Forces beyond the physical world I was trying to save. Forces even more divine than the Lady of the Lake, but that was another story. There were more immediate concerns than contemplating the meaning of life.

"What will become of you?" I asked the Lady. "Will you stay in Avalon for eternity?"

"If I leave Avalon, I will most certainly die, but one day, my Light will fade and cease to be. Either way, there will be an end."

"And Morgana?"

"Her power grows, even as we speak. I'm bound, but she is not."

"So she can live forever." I sighed. *Typical.* "Is she the only one?"

"Through the chaos of the ages, only three of us remain."

I blinked, the news surprising me. "There are three Celestials? Where is the third?"

"She is bound to her world by her own misfortune. She cannot transcend."

"You sound sad about it."

"Battles rage all around us. That is the fate of our physical forms. We live forever, destined to watch those we love die, unable to follow to the next life. She is my likeness, yet we will never meet. There is a sadness in that, don't you think?"

"I guess you're right," I murmured.

I opened my hand and studied the white flower, knowing that the fight for Earth was left in the Naturals hands once more. The petals seemed to sparkle behind the shard of crystal, and I wondered how such a small thing could hold so much power.

"How am I supposed to use it?" I asked. "It's so delicate."

"When the time comes, all will be revealed."

I groaned and fastened the chain around my neck. "How did I know you were going to say that?"

"I will be watching," the Lady of the Lake told me, her smile full of a strange knowing. "If I can help, I will."

I grimaced and turned towards the valley. *But don't count on it.*

"You better send me back to the Druid homeland," I declared. "I've got work to do."

The Lady of the Lake waved her hand though the air, opening a portal that shone with pure white starlight.

"Good luck, Madeleine Greenbriar," she said. "May the Light of Avalon guide you to victory."

18

I stepped out of the portal and emerged in the centre of Brionglóid henge.

Elijah was leaning against one of the huge grey and black stones, and smiled as he saw me appear.

As the portal closed behind me with a *snap*, I went to meet him, glad he was here. "Have you been waiting all this time?"

"It wasn't that long," he replied, pushing off the stone. "I spoke to Merlin for a while, then wandered down the hill. I just got here, actually. It's been half an hour since you left."

I blinked, dazed. "But it felt like I was in Avalon for hours..."

Elijah winked. "That's the cost of bending time and space for you."

Fading into thought, I attempted to wrap my mind around the puzzle that was Avalon. It was impossible. Maybe my mind was too small to comprehend more than what my eyes could see. Even a Triune had her limits, I supposed.

"Are you up for a walk?" Elijah asked, slipping his hand into mine.

His touch drew me back to the present and I nodded. "I have a lot to tell you. The Lady of the Lake sure knows how to talk."

"Well, she is in Avalon all alone. A new face must have been refreshing."

"I don't know," I mused. "She seemed to know things."

"Another Celestial mystery?"

"It was like she watched the world through a window."

Elijah snorted. "Well, I hope she doesn't watch me in the shower."

"*Erm…*" I choked on my own spit and straightened my tunic.

"Don't worry," he said with a laugh. "I think ogling naked Druids is a little beyond someone like her."

We left the henge together, passing underneath one of the lintels. Crossing over a break in the ditch, Elijah led me into the forest where a thin trail carved a path through the thick woods.

I noticed the white flowers grew here too, poking their heads out of the grass and shaking their proverbial fists at me. Now I realised what they were, I wondered if the Druids did, too.

They wore them in their hair, wove them in their rituals, and allowed them to bloom over everything, even amongst the stones of Brionglóid. They had to, right?

"Forget-me-nots!" I exclaimed. "I thought they were familiar."

"Forget who?" Elijah asked. "I don't get it."

"The flowers. They grow on Earth in all kinds of colours," I told him. "These are the same but are pure white with a little yellow centre. They represent…" I clicked my fingers together, trying to think, "true love. *That's it.*"

Of course. It always came back to true love with the Celestials. The Twin Flames had to merge with it in their hearts to defeat the One and it was jealous love that triggered the cataclysm in the first place. Why would Morgana be any different?

I just wish I knew what it meant when it came to using the flower on her.

"We have stories that say the Celestials gifted us with them," Elijah said. "They're special, that's why we let them grow wherever they sprout."

"It makes sense, then. The Lady of the Lake said they grew where her people walked. She showed me." I pulled the crystal out from beneath my tunic and held it up so he could see. "This is what's going to help us defeat Morgana."

He blinked and narrowed his eyes at the pendant. "A flower?"

"That's what I said. Exactly like that, too."

"I bet she said you'd know how to use it when the time came, as well."

I gasped dramatically and stifled a laugh. "How did you know?"

Elijah shrugged. "She *is* best friends with Merlin."

"Of course. Now we know where he gets it from…or is it the other way around?"

"You seem more at ease," Elijah said as we walked. "Did you get all the answers we were hoping for?"

"She had a lot to say," I told him. "About how she came to be, the other Celestials—did you know there's another one?"

"A third Celestial?"

"The Lady said the third is trapped in her own world. She seemed to think she was good, like her."

"Awesome. I don't think I could deal with another cranky Celestial."

I raised my eyebrows and chuckled.

"What?" he asked. "It's the truth."

"Yeah, it's just weird hearing you say awesome. Especially when you're dressed like you're going to a renaissance fair."

He wrapped his arm around my waist and tugged me close. "Look who's talking."

As we strolled through the forest, I told Elijah everything the Lady of the Lake had revealed—about Morgana and the creation of the Dark, her beginnings as a 'born' Celestial, why she couldn't leave Avalon, the truth of Merlin and the Darklands, and more about the flower she'd given me. I also tried to describe her as best I could, but I couldn't find the right words.

"That's a lot to take in," Elijah mused. "What she said about Merlin and the Darklands explains a lot."

"And why he's so old and still so spritely."

"I fear his pact may come back to haunt him, though."

I paused, causing Elijah to take another step without me. "How so?"

"To protect the homeland, he'll have to live forever. Unless he can hand the mantle on to someone else. Druids live a long time, but forever is a huge burden."

I frowned, wondering if Merlin had asked a price for Elijah's Colours, if this would have been it.

He nodded down the path, oblivious to my thoughts. "C'mon. I want to show you something."

Thankful for the distraction, I followed. The forest thickened, then thinned as we came upon a stream. A massive tree drooped over the edge, trailing its leaves in the fast-moving water.

It was a willow, just like the one he'd been hiding in inside his mind. The similarities made me shiver, but it was only a simple tree, wasn't it?

"A willow," I murmured, my gaze flickering to the stream that bubbled and gurgled behind it.

"The willow symbolises the connection between the earth and sky," Elijah explained. "More specifically, between water and the moon. It is a place where Druids meditate on the connection between life and spirit."

"This is where you've been calling your Colours?"

He nodded and tugged on my hand, guiding me

underneath the drooping branches. We stepped into a private world, shielded by a wall of green, and I could feel the power encased in the tree. It was a little bubble of essence.

We sat on the grass, our legs touching. My heart thrummed, but I wasn't sure if it was from his closeness or the energy flowing through the willow. We hadn't had a quiet moment together in such a long time. At least, not like this…away from prying eyes.

"Our time here is coming to an end," he began. "We have our answers…"

I swallowed hard, the flower weighing heavily around my neck. Things were taking a serious turn. Elijah was right when he'd said he felt like something was coming to an end.

It was time for us to choose our fates.

"I was at Castle Brent the day Wilder and Scarlett went into the rift," I began. "The castle had been abandoned by the Naturals of Camelot for hundreds of years, and everything was crumbling and smelt like rotting wood. The defences were useless, but we reinforced them with Light, patching holes and digging trenches outside. I was just as useless, of course. I was mutated then, almost completely Dark." I lowered my gaze, remembering the looks I'd been given while I sat in a corner, trying to make myself as small as possible. "While the Flames fought Mordred at Camelot, we were facing a horde of demons outside the castle. I'll never forget the Darkness that swarmed towards the walls. Infected and possessed humans and Naturals swarmed the castle and we were forced to fight or die. How do you drive a sword through your own kind? How do you justify taking their lives so you can save your own?"

"Madeleine," Elijah said placing his hand on my thigh. "It was an impossible situation."

"I just… This is going to end the same way. I can feel it," I murmured. "The odds were against us with the demons, and they might be a shadow of what they once were, but now they have Morgana. An *immortal* Celestial being." I felt the crystal press against my skin under my tunic. "And all that stands in her way is a flower. *A bloody flower.*"

"I believe in you, Madeleine. I believe in us," he said. "And Greer and the others. Together, we can stand against her."

"It's not that. I"

His hand felt heavy on my leg and I resisted the urge to push him away. How could ask him to come with me when we only had a one percent chance of winning? Thríbhís Mhór was his home.

"Madeleine, what are you saying?"

"There'll always be another war to fight," I told him. "We're the only people with the power to stand against the unknown and protect our worlds. That's my destiny and always will be. I can't ask you to shoulder that burden for a world that's not yours. I've asked so much of you already."

Elijah's gaze searched mine. "You never had to ask."

"I can never repay you for what you've given me,"

I said, my throat tightening with emotion. "Acceptance, faith, trust..." My tongue thickened before I could say the word love, and my heart began to crack.

I still couldn't say it, but Elijah deserved to hear the truth if he was going to make the right decision for his future. I had to get over myself and my fears, just like I'd promised the Old Ones.

"Madeleine—"

"I know I'm a mess and I don't know my mind from my heart half the time," I rambled. "And sometimes I do the opposite of what I say, and I rush into danger without thinking. And I'm rebellious and reckless and more trouble than I'm worth, but I love you, Elijah." I looked at my hands, desperately fighting back tears. "But you also deserve to be with your people. I can't take that away from you. You'd have a life of peace and understanding I could never give you. I just..." I swallowed the lump in my throat, "I just thought you deserved to know before I left, was all."

Elijah slid his palm around my wrist. "All of those things—the fighting, the danger, the politics, the prejudices—they don't matter. But you and me?" He shook his head and to my astonishment, his Colours flared. "No matter which world you are in, Madeleine Greenbriar, what I feel for you will never change."

My skin tingled and I looked down to see delicate blue threads crawling up my arm. They wove a complex pattern, all sharp angles shimmering with holographic light. It was the same as when I'd stood before him in his mind, when he'd been freed of the Dark.

He was declaring his love for me in the deepest way a Druid could, but this time, it was real.

"*Elijah…*"

I pushed up my sleeve and my breath caught as the prism flared and sunk into my skin before it disappeared. Unlike the last time, I felt the threads tingle all the way to the bone and travel all the way to my spirit.

"I won't leave you," he whispered. "*I can't*, prism or no prism. You and I are bound."

The world fell away, and all I could see was Elijah. Was this what true love felt like? An unbearable pain that could only be sated by his kiss? I didn't know, but I wrapped my arms around his neck and pressed my lips to his.

Our touch deepened, my hands moving to places they'd never been before. I was full of boldness— facing my truth had filled me with a confidence I never knew I had. Embarrassment over such things seemed silly now that I was here with Elijah… entangled and aflame.

"Are you sure?" he whispered, his breath hot on my skin.

"*Yes.*" Nothing else seemed to matter. Whatever happened next, we would always have this moment.

"Madeleine, my *leannán…*"

Afterwards, as we lay together under the willow, I sighed.

"I didn't know it would be like that," I murmured, watching the sunlight dapple through the branches.

"When you love someone," Elijah told me, the prism flaring on my arm, "that's how it's supposed to be."

19

E lijah and I were barely dressed when a screech tore through the air, piercing the bubble around the willow tree.

I clapped my hands over my ears as my soul reacted, shuddering and threatening to overcome me. Elijah held me steady.

"What in the world?" I hissed as it subsided.

"Something's wrong," he said, parting the branches and peering out into the forest.

"What was that sound?"

"I don't know."

I pushed past him. "We have to get back to the village."

We ran all the way back to Brionglóid henge, but Merlin was nowhere to be found. The stone circle was empty, though the crystal in the rock was humming. The low note sounded like fingernails scratching on a chalkboard and I winced.

Elijah paused. "Are you okay?"

"Something is screwing with me," I replied.

"I can't feel anything…" He cursed as the ground began to shake. The henge shuddered, the stones groaned around us as they moved with the shockwaves.

"*The village.*" I pointed to the path, dead rising thick and fast.

Pushing past the pain, I followed Elijah.

As we reached the rise and the first cottages came into view, I skidded to a complete stop, looking down at the carnage.

A creature made of pure indigo was rampaging on the outskirts of the village, crushing everything in its path. Horrified screams echoed up the hill as Druids fled and those who were strong enough attempted to cage it with Colour.

A relic. No wonder the stones at the henge were reacting.

"*Holy…* Is that what I think it is?" I cried. "*Why does everything have to be so hard?*"

It was larger than the one we'd fought in the Darklands—I estimated it was thirteen feet tall…then there were its antlers. Rotting skin hung from the twisted bone and it shed as it rammed into buildings.

Its hide was so black, it seemed to suck in any light it touched, and its eyes burned with a fierce silver light that had echoes of the other side—death, otherwise known as the spirit world.

Elijah was just as stunned as I was. "What the hell is a relic doing here?"

"Why is it attacking the homeland?" I exclaimed,

my heart galloping a wild beat. "Shouldn't it be guarding it?"

"It shouldn't have been able to cross," he replied. "Something let it in."

"Or *someone*."

"*Morgana*," he hissed. "Merlin would never break the pact with the Old Ones."

"This is bad," I muttered. No wonder my soul was affected—the Dark part of me was calling to her. "*So very bad.*"

"They'll need our help," Elijah said. "C'mon."

Together, we sprinted through the village towards the massive creature. Druids scattered around us, carrying children and helping the elderly, clearing out of the village as quickly as they were able.

Skidding to a stop between two cottages, we stared up at the monster, our mouths agape. In full sunlight, and up close, the relic was even more terrifying than it had been in the Darklands.

The head of a wolf, the antlers of a stag, the body of a lion, fuelled by the power of ancient gods. *We were screwed.*

A trail of destruction lay in its wake. Clawed hands and feet had torn up the ground and antlers carved holes into buildings. Fire had taken hold of a watched roof, smoke billowing into the air.

The *neach-gleidhidh* poured out of the village and surrounded the beast, weaponless but dressed for battle. Holding their hands high, their Colours flared and shimmering blue threads arced into the sky, casting a geometric net around the massive creature.

The relic roared, throwing its head back, and galloped towards the prism. Its antlers collided with the web and it fell onto its haunches, dazed.

Eliorla came to meet us as Elijah and I snapped out of our daze. "Caradhan, Madeleine, have you seen Merlin?" she asked. "Was he with you at Brionglóid?"

"He won't be able to do anything," I said with a moan. "The Lady of the Lake…"

"What are you talking about?" the Druidess demanded.

"Merlin is bound to the Darklands. He—"

"*Mac soith*," she cursed.

The prism wavered and I reached for my arondight blade. It was at my hip, where it hadn't left despite being in a place that was supposed to be peaceful. I guess it was just habit. I didn't even feel the weight of it, and no one had said anything, not even Merlin or the Lady of the Lake. I had a feeling they could have stopped me without breaking a sweat if my Dark side chose to go rogue.

"Why aren't they fighting back?" I exclaimed in frustration.

"We can't," Elijah replied. "The relic is part of the Darklands."

"And the Darklands are a part of the Old Ones." I groaned and drew my arondight hilt. "Looks like I'm the woman for the job."

"We need two swords," he added. "I'll come with you."

Eliorla grabbed his arm and wrenched him back.

"Caradhan, if you go against the Darklands, you will never be able to return."

"That's my choice to make, sister."

She looked aghast. "You're going to abandon us for the Triune? Your own people?"

"No. I'm not just doing it for her. I'm doing it to save my people from Morgana. I don't belong here, Eliorla. I'm a Druid, I always will be, but my destiny lies in another world."

I placed my palm on his chest. "You may be coming with me, but I won't allow you to close off your only way home. Forever is a long time."

"But—"

I pressed my fingers to his lips. "*Trust me.*"

Elijah froze, neither agreeing nor arguing.

The only way to kill the relic was to pierce both of its hearts at precisely the same time. I didn't know how I was going to do it on my own, but I was going to give it my best shot.

I turned to Eliorla. "Can you and your warriors contain it?"

Eliorla nodded. "We can weave a prism around it, but it won't hold for long."

"Hopefully, I won't need much time. We just have to keep it away from the village."

"To the north, beyond the farmland is a wild meadow," she told me. "If the Celestial is controlling it, the *réalta flùr*—the flowers—should weaken her hold." So they did know about the forget-me-nots. *Réalta flùr* seemed to be a mix of Scottish Gaelic and Irish. *Star flowers.*

"And no Druids will be harmed," I said. "Good."

The relic let out a roar that rattled the windows of the surrounding cottages. The Druids holding it back stumbled and their barrier flared and nearly flickered out.

Elijah grasped my arm. "*Madeleine.*"

"Give me your arondight blade," I commanded, not wanting to hear him plead to let him come. "I know you're carrying it." I had a hand in undressing him earlier after all.

He reached under his shirt and took the hilt off his belt and reluctantly handed it to me.

I grasped Eliorla's arm and held her steely gaze with my own—emerald eyes and grey. "I'm going to draw it north," I told her. "Get ready to follow."

She nodded sharply. "Good luck, *Trí Anam.*"

"Madeleine." Elijah stepped in front of me. "*I love you.*"

I smiled and traced the curve of his jaw. "I love you, too."

Before he could convince me to stay, I darted back the way we came, ghosting through the village. I circled around the relic and approached it from behind. I had to lead it away from the settlement without destroying it in the process.

I passed through the prism and the relic turned, baring its teeth when it saw me. Was that recognition in its eyes? Was Morgana watching us through it? I hoped so, because when I cut it down, *I wanted her to see.*

In its presence, I was a mere speck. The monster

towered over everything and I began to wonder if this was such a good idea. I'd fought a Colossus before—a chimera made of Darkness and human flesh—but this was worse.

"You've got a lot of nerve coming here," I said, narrowing my eyes. "It's time to go for a run. Won't that be fun? Will you look at that! *I rhymed.*"

The prism began to fade and then it was gone.

The relic seemed to smile—if baring its razor-sharp teeth at me was its way of expressing triumph—and took a step towards me. All it had to do was snap its jaws and I'd be lunch.

I waved my fingers at it. "Bye, arsehole."

I took off, sprinting through the edge of the village towards the farmland to the north. The relic let out a strangled cry and the ground shook as it gave pursuit. Crashes echoed as it collided with buildings and fences in its desperation to catch me.

I leapt over a stone wall into a field, not brave enough to look back. I didn't have to see the monster to know it was right behind me. Its presence was like a sickness in the air, the stench permitting everything, even the places it hadn't been yet. The wind could have been blowing away from it and I still would have gagged at the rot it carried.

What were the Old Ones thinking when they created a beast like this? Had they made it or was it just a product of the world it came from? Right now, it was it or me.

No prizes for guessing who I wanted to win.

I hurdled over another fence and crashed through

a small patch of woodland before I emerged into another field. This one was dotted with thousands of white flowers—the meadow.

I kept running, my boots thudding as my power propelled me forwards, not stopping until I reached the far side.

The relic lingered at the tree line, frothing at the mouth as it hesitated. Eliorla was right—it didn't like the flowers—but even as we both lingered, I knew it wouldn't hang back for long. Morgana wanted me too much. After what I'd done in Edinburgh, she knew I was the only one strong enough to stand against her.

The relic growled, its eyes blazed as it advanced. Every step it took, steam rose from its hands and feet like the flowers were burning its putrid flesh.

Backing away, my gaze studied the lay of the land. I had it kill it before it killed me. I wasn't immortal and neither were the Druids.

Two hearts, two swords.

I tensed as the relic rose to its full height. Black eyes pierced my grey and I knew it was death or glory.

Have faith, Madeleine. You can do this.

I sprinted towards the beast and it galloped towards me, its claws carving up the earth and tossing clumps of grass into the air. It lowered its head, aiming its antlers and protecting its chest. Bone dug into the ground, tearing a destructive path straight towards me.

I was not afraid.

I reached inside myself as deep as I could go and let my power flow freely. I was once afraid of losing control and destroying Camelot and the world along with it. I'd called forth fire from the earth itself to stop Ikakantor from storming the castle, and I'd calmed the ancient volcano underneath Edinburgh. What was a relic compared to that?

Light, Dark, and Colour flowed into the swords, igniting the blades with a rainbow of flame.

I had less than a split-second to make a decision. *Up or down…*

I skidded, my boots digging into the soft earth and my arse scraping behind, and I struck. Metal collided with bone, slicing through the relic's right antler and severing it completely.

The beast roared and toppled, its head smashing into the ground. The force of the collision sent the creature's back end flying up into the air. Fortunately, I had my angles right and skidded underneath its left antler.

The tip of the rotting bone brushed my cheek as the relic tumbled, and the moment I was clear, I pushed against the ground and into the air. I twisted, propelled by a burst of essence, and flipped the arondight blades around.

The monster landed on its back and began to slide across the meadow, its chest exposed. I hurtled downwards, not sure if I was going to make it in time.

The blades sank into flesh and the relic screamed, its voice vibrating through my bones and clawing at my psyche, and I knew…

I missed.

I cried out as black blood stung my exposed skin

and pulled the swords free. The relic thrashed and I almost fell, but a flare of Colour surrounded us, holding the beast steady.

Eliorla.

My gaze met hers as the keepers surrounded the relic, and she nodded. Her expression said it all. *Strike.*

I flipped the swords in my hands, grasping the hilts, and plunged them into the relic. Metal cut through blackened flesh, striking deep and true.

The echo of the beast's heartbeats pulsed up the blades, rasping against my soul. A tortured scream ripped through Thríbhís Mhór, the sound shaking everything it reached.

Just as suddenly as it began, the sound cut off and the relic slackened. Its flesh began to bubble and spit, melting away from bone.

I let the swords return to their hilts and jumped back to solid ground, holding my sleeve over my nose. *Ugh*, it stunk like Sulphur mixed with death.

When the flesh was gone, creepy empty skeleton eyes stared at me, then that too began to crumble.

The last of the creature sank into the earth, leaving behind a bare patch of earth, but as I stood there, green began to sprout. Brilliant emerald grass reached for the sky and tiny white flowers began to unfurl, creeping along the churned meadow, reclaiming what the relic had destroyed.

I wiped the back of my hand across my face, my skin stinging where the relic's blood had burned. *What a ride.*

"*Mo bandia*," Eliorla whispered as the rest of the keepers crowded around us.

"You were right," I told her. "The flowers helped."

She smiled, and I knew I'd finally won her over. "Never have I seen such a fierce warrior. Thank you, *Trí Anam*."

The Druids reached out, each brushing their fingertips against my arms. I didn't know what it was supposed to mean, but it seemed to be some kind of gesture of thanks. That's what I wanted to believe anyway, because *bandia* meant goddess in Irish and I wasn't sure how much of their language mixed with that and Scots Gaelic. She could be calling me a toaster for all I knew.

"What happened to it?" I asked the Druids.

"Thríbhís Mhór has purified it," Eliorla replied. "It did not belong here."

"*Madeleine!*"

Elijah sprinted across the meadow and collided with me, his arms wrapping around my body. I still tingled from what we'd shared under the willow and the power I'd unleashed on the relic as I sank against him.

After a moment of indulgence, I drew back and grinned up at him. "*Told you so*."

"I understand now," Eliorla said, but it wasn't clear if she was talking about my intentions as a Triune or Elijah's feelings.

As we stood there, I sensed the presence of the villagers gathering around the meadow. They'd come to see what had become of the relic, and their curiosity sang to my Colours.

It was a moment of triumph, but I feared the relic was only the beginning.

Another world had been added to Morgana's hit list and I held the key to everyone's survival. A white flower was the only thing standing between Morgana and the death of Earth and Thríbhís Mhór. That such a small thing could seal our fate…

Morgana must die. There was no other way.

"So," I said, wiping my bloody palms on my trousers, "any chance of a bath? This stuff stings."

20

Back in our little cottage, I dipped a cloth into a basin of water and sighed.

Elijah was fussing with a change of clothes, inspecting the gear we'd brought with us from Earth. He was preparing for our imminent return while I remained covered in relic blood.

It seemed like I hadn't had a chance to take a breath in a long time.

"Eliorla called me *Trí Anam*," I said. "What does it mean?"

"Three soul is the literal translation," Elijah replied. "It's the Druid's way of saying Triune."

I smiled. "Well, it's better than being called a *mèirleach*. Though I wish you Druids would make up your mind between Irish and Scots. I can't keep up."

"Some words are prettier than others," he reasoned.

I put it out of my mind and turned back to the

basin and stripped off my stained tunic. Elijah stood behind me and reached for the damp cloth.

"Your skin is burned," he murmured, dabbing it across my shoulders.

"The relic's blood must be corrosive," I replied, fully aware that I was half-naked in front of him. It no longer felt embarrassing for him to see me like this, but thrilling. "The burns seem to be healing."

"That they are," he replied, smoothing his palms over my shoulders. "I can get another cloth if you want to return the favour."

"*Elijah…*"

He chuckled and handed it back to me. "By the way… Can I have my sword back?"

I burst out laughing as the tension bled from the room. "Only if you stop being so wicked."

"But it's so fun," he complained.

The crystal dangled around my neck, the chain seeming to drag against my skin. Was it making its presence known? I sure as hell didn't need the reminder that the fight with the relic was the calm before the extinction-level event.

"Are you sure?" I asked, turning to face Elijah.

He kept his gaze on mine, sensing the change in my demeanour. "About?"

"Leaving."

"Yes," he said, touching my arm. The prism flared, then settled back into my skin. "*With all my soul.*"

Eliorla and the keepers were assisting with the clean-up efforts when Elijah and I emerged from the cottage.

We were ready to depart for the Darklands, our arondight blades holstered, cold iron daggers sheathed, and our Natural uniforms in place. It seemed too soon.

"There is much to do," Eliorla told me when I asked about the rebuilding. "Until Merlin returns, I'm not sure how to proceed with patrolling the borders. The Darklands are unpredictable under the best of circumstances."

"Merlin hasn't come back yet?" I asked. "Do you think…?"

"It's only been a few hours," Elijah said. "He'll—"

"*Merlin*," Eliorla gasped, falling to her knees. "*Tá brón orm.*" The keepers followed suit, kneeling as the old Druid approached, melting out of the forest like a spectre.

Talk about abrupt and unexpected entrances.

"Rise, Eliorla. There are no apologies needed here." He studied the damage to the village, his brow creased. "I could not stop the breach. I was bound and Morgana knew it."

"We tried to force it back into the Darklands," the Druidess said, "but it was too powerful. The portal would not open."

"The Celestial was in control," Elijah said to her. "It wasn't your fault."

Merlin turned his gaze on me. He seemed to

already know what I'd done without me even admitting it.

"I killed the relic," I told him. "I took the burden so your people didn't upset the balance with the Darklands. It's the only thing protecting you." I glanced back towards the meadow. "Well, it was."

"I see you are prepared for battle."

I nodded. "We have a matter to settle with a certain Celestial. We have to go back to Earth and face her before more damage is done…to both our worlds."

"The Old Ones won't allow you to stay in the Darklands unchallenged," Merlin warned. "You have angered them by killing the relic."

"Then we'll have to run," I told him. The only way to get to the homeland was through the Darklands. When I left, I would never be able to return, but I took comfort knowing Elijah could come back one day. "There's still the question of the portal back to Earth."

"We can open it," Elijah said. "And run together."

"But your Colours have only just started to reappear," Eliorla argued.

"I have enough Colour to join with Madeleine's. We'll only have one chance, though."

"The Celestial could be waiting for you, even now," the Druidess said.

"Then let her come." I pressed my palm against the crystal flower underneath my shirt. "The Lady of the Lake granted us a lifeline and I intend to use it the first chance I get."

Eliorla looked me over with a grimace that seemed to be her version of showing respect. "I do not doubt it, *Trí Anam.*"

Merlin spoke then, causing us all to fall silent. He had that way about him. "If you are set on returning, Caradhan, then be warned. Without a connection to Thríbhís Mhór, your Colours may overwhelm you. They have been subdued for a long time and their return will be unpredictable."

"What does that mean?" I asked, glancing at Elijah. "You never said…"

"I didn't want to worry you," he murmured. "It's nothing really."

"I have guided you as much as I can," Merlin said to him. "If it happens, there is nothing to be done but wait for you to work your way through the knot."

"I understand. I know the risks, but our fight against Morgana is the greater threat. I am as much part of Earth as I am the homeland."

"Then it is settled," Merlin said. "Caradhan, it is time to say your goodbyes. Madeleine, would you walk with me?"

"Now?" I glanced at Elijah, but he'd already turned to his sister.

Merlin threaded his arm through mine, the gesture taking me by surprise. He led me away from the siblings and through the village. As we walked, various Druids paused to speak a few words to him. He apologised for his absence and listened when they aired their grievances.

Being a leader to a people who'd lost so much was

a difficult reality. I wasn't sure I'd be able to handle it with as much grace as Merlin did.

"It seems too soon," I said after a while. "It doesn't feel right leaving while there's so much damage to repair."

"Are you referring to the village, or Caradhan?"

I sighed and lowered my gaze. "He just found his sister. A handful of days is hardly enough to make up for eight hundred years."

"Goodbyes are difficult," he said. "They part, knowing they may not see each other again, but glad they had the chance to meet…even for such a brief time."

"I'm worried he's making the wrong choice," I admitted. "I love him, but a part of me feels selfish for wanting him to come with me. I'm taking him to a battlefield where he could ultimately die."

"Love and sacrifice walk hand-in-hand," Merlin stated. "This is Caradhan's way of declaring his love for not only you, but his people."

I sighed, still feeling awful that Elijah would have to leave his home after trying for so long to find his way back.

Merlin sensed my turmoil. "You have a good heart, Madeleine Greenbriar, despite the Darkness you carry."

I blinked. "Thanks, I guess."

We took a turn around the village, passing by the churned farmland the relic had galloped through. Men and women were busy replanting and salvaging what they could from the crop.

"The relics will keep breaching the way between your worlds, won't they?" I asked.

"Yes," Merlin replied. "Once you and Caradhan leave, I must sever Thríbhís Mhór from the Darklands to prevent another attack. It's a temporary measure, but nothing will be able to pass through the veil while I hold it, not even Morgana."

"Temporary?"

Merlin smiled. "Eventually the Darklands will bleed through again, but that is my burden."

"The Lady told me about your pact with the Old Ones."

"Ah," he said, inclining his head, "I see."

"It's the worst-kept secret, I'm afraid. Eliorla is aware of your connection to the Old Ones, and after you were absent when the relic attacked, everyone else is, too."

The old Druid sighed, lost in an unknown memory. Thinking about the life he must have led struck me with an awe I'd never felt before. He'd walked Earth, the Druid homeland, and the Darklands for a thousand years or more, and who knew how many other worlds. The things he'd seen, the trials he'd faced, and the knowledge he held were unfathomable.

If anyone could face Morgana, it was him. But he had his own people to protect and he'd bound himself to them through the pact he'd made with the Old Ones. There was no leaving for him. *Ever.*

"The world is changing, Madeleine," he said.

"Mine and yours. Even the threads binding them together are fraying."

"Then we just have to weave them together again."

The Druid laughed, his beard fluttering in the breeze. "I saw you at the helm of that loom."

I pouted. "It's a figure of speech."

"Fortunately for us."

I shook my head, not quite believing I was *bantering* with Merlin like we were old friends catching up over a drink or two.

"Oh, to be young again," he murmured. "I would go with you in a heartbeat, my child. It's a cruel twist of fate that I ask you to be the champion of not only the Druids, but the Naturals, too."

"I understand," I told him. "We all have our parts to play in destiny."

He smiled in that creepy all-knowing way he had and declared, "Sometimes, destiny needs a little outside interference."

When we returned to the edge of the village, Elijah and Eliorla were waiting for us.

"Are you ready?" he asked.

"I don't think I'll ever be ready," I told him. "But now is as good a time as any, I suppose."

He grinned. "That's the spirit."

Merlin swept his hands through the air and I felt his power reach out to the veil. A portal opened, swirling like a whirlpool of rippling grey. Colour shimmered across the surface and I could make out the faint outline of the Darklands beyond. He made it look so easy compared to my parents' wired contraception of crystals and batteries.

My parents. Were they still alive? Were they safe? It was time to go back and make things right.

Eliorla held up her hand. "Farewell, *Trí Anam*," she said. "*Madeleine.* Look after my thick-headed brother, will you?"

I smiled and nodded. "It will be my pleasure."

Elijah took my hand and we turned towards the portal. The Darklands shimmered beyond, the crystalline landscape promising a rough ride ahead.

We stepped through, knowing we had moments before we needed to run for our lives.

I glanced over my shoulder, giving Thríbhís Mhór and the Druids one last look as the portal began to shrink. Merlin's gaze met mine and I almost heard his voice echo across time.

Slán, Trí Anam. Ádh mór. Farewell, Triune. Good luck…

The portal snapped closed behind us, sealing the Druid homeland. Now, the race was on.

Earth, and Morgana, awaited.

OTHER BOOKS IN THE CAMELOT ARCHIVE
by Nicole R. Taylor

Demon Bound #1
Demon Sworn #2
Demon Forged #3
Demon Eternal #4

Go back to where it all began:
THE ARONDIGHT CODEX

An ancient war with demons. A lost sword with the power to end it all. And a woman with purple hair is the world's only hope.

Dark Descent #1
Dark Illusion #2
Dark Abandon #3
Dark Genesis #4
Dark Crucible #5

ABOUT NICOLE

Nicole R. Taylor is an Australian Urban Fantasy author.

She lives in the western suburbs of Melbourne dreaming up nail biting stories featuring sassy witches, duplicitous vampires, hunky shapeshifters, and devious monsters.

She likes chocolate, cat memes, and video games.

When she's not writing, she likes to think of what she's writing next.

Follow Nicole Online:

Website: www.nicolertaylorwrites.com
Facebook: facebook.com/nrtaylorwrites
Newsletter: www.nicolertaylorwrites.com/newsletter
Email: nicole.this.is@gmail.com

DEMON ETERNAL (THE CAMELOT ARCHIVE - BOOK FOUR)

A SNEAK PEEK...

CHAPTER ONE

Silver light shone down on the Darklands, casting long shadows over the nightmarish landscape.

Elijah and I ran through the crystalline maze, weaving around the enormous obsidian and smokey quartz points, our boots crunching against crumbled gemstones. I felt the eyes of the Old Ones on my back, their anger burning into my flesh. I'd killed one of their creatures and now I was an outlaw in a lawless land.

Only hours ago, the Celestial Morgana had pushed a relic—a fearsome predator with the head of a wolf, the antlers of a stag, and the body of a lion—through the veil into the Druid homeland where it proceeded to destroy everything in its path. I'd had two choices—let it carve through the Druid's homeland or kill it. I'd done what any warrior,

Natural or otherwise, would have done—I stabbed it through its twin hearts.

Now we were on the way home, forced to run for our lives because of my actions. If I'd let Elijah help, he would have broken the pact between the Druids and the Old Ones and been exiled for it. My place would always be on Earth, so it seemed worth the cost, despite our current flight through the Darklands.

Now, it was run or die.

There were creatures other than relics who patrolled this lightless place—shadows, spirits, and monsters so ancient no one had ever laid eyes on them. I could sense them all around, watching us, lingering just beyond the pale.

We paused at the edge of the rugged maze to catch our breath. The air was thick and the atmosphere pushed down on our shoulders like boulders. Everything was harder, even my abilities seemed a little farther away than usual.

I pressed my palm against stone, but it was cold to the touch. Like last time, I couldn't feel any warmth in this world. It teemed with dangerous life, even though scarce light touched its surface.

The laws that governed life as we knew it didn't seem to hold here and it made things all the more uncertain.

"Do we have to go as far as the forest?" I murmured, glancing at Elijah. It had taken us two days to find our way to Thríbhís Mhór, and I was dreading the way back.

"We can't just open the portal from anywhere," he

reminded me. "We could end up on an alternate Earth…or inside a wall."

"So, it's back to the hill or nowhere at all."

He nodded. "We're making good time."

"Your Colours?"

He'd only just begun to recover them after the ritual at Brionglóid Henge in the Druid homeland, Thríbhís Mhór. It would take time before they returned completely, but that was the thing about our predicament—we didn't have time to wait.

"They'll hold," he replied. "We just have to get the portal open."

Morgana was still out there and there was no telling when she might pop up. An immortal, borderline insane Celestial being was after us. It was Earth or bust. *Literally*.

"Can you feel that?" I rubbed my hand over the back of my neck and shivered.

Elijah scanned the forest ahead. "We better keep moving."

An enraged roar echoed from the maze behind us and we took off, not wanting to be anywhere near the crystals when the relics caught up to us. One was bad enough, but two? Three? A whole horde? Running sounded like a good idea.

We broke through the tree line and began to pick our way through the tangled woodland. Our progress was slow, hampered by centuries of unhindered growth. We'd traded one maze for another, but at least this one was familiar despite the black hue.

Hours passed, and I almost believed we were

going to pass unhindered when my power began to zap through my veins. I was picking up on something that was growing in the shadows—figures, spirits, the empty husks known as the Unworthy.

Remembering our first trip here, and the lost souls the Darklands had claimed for its shadow army, I quickened my steps to catch up with Elijah.

He faltered in front of me and I knew he felt them, too. Still, I did the one thing people shouldn't do when they sensed something with murderous intent was stalking them.

I looked back.

Shadows swarmed after us like a thick cloud, wrapping around trees, oozing through gaps we had no hope of passing.

This was bad, but not just any bad. It was the *ultimate bad*.

We bolted, driven forwards by a primal need for survival. We hadn't come this far only to become empty husks.

Ahead, Elijah skidded as the shadow people poured over our path. He made a sharp right then leapt over a fallen log. I followed, my palm scraping on black lichen as I vaulted over the decaying tree.

There was no time to think, to cry out, to ask if he knew the way back to the hill. The shadows were on our tail and one misstep could see us overwhelmed. All we could do was run for our lives.

We swatted away thick vines and ducked underneath low hanging branches. I clambered over protruding roots and sharp rocks. We slipped along slimy black moss. Our breath quickened as the shadows closed in on us.

Just when I thought we'd become lost, we broke into clear ground, our boots thudding on springy pitch-coloured grass. Ahead, the ground began to rise into a clear sky.

The hill.

"Open the portal," I shouted to Elijah. "I'll hold them back!" He glanced over his shoulder, his eyes wild. *"I'm right behind you."*

Turning, I threw up my hands and cast a web of Light towards our pursuers. Gold shimmered brightly as the lost souls collided with it. The force of their blows shook the web, nearly knocking me over.

I felt Elijah call on his Colours, coaxing the portal to form, but without joining with my Druid Triune it wouldn't open completely.

Shadows gathered around my Light, scraping and clawing, sucking the power from my fingertips. I was keeping them from overwhelming us, but in doing so, I was giving them exactly what they needed to grow stronger.

We just needed enough time to open the portal. *Just a few more moments…*

Demon Eternal is OUT NOW!